"The Guardians of The Scroll"

by

Georgina Thomas

Bloomington, IN Milton Keynes, UK

authorHOUSE®

AuthorHouse™
1663 Liberty Drive, Suite 200
Bloomington, IN 47403
www.authorhouse.com
Phone: 1-800-839-8640

AuthorHouse™ UK Ltd.
500 Avebury Boulevard
Central Milton Keynes, MK9 2BE
www.authorhouse.co.uk
Phone: 08001974150

First published by AuthorHouse 10/11/2006

ISBN: 1-4259-4575-9 (sc)

Printed in the United States of America
Bloomington, Indiana

This book is printed on acid-free paper.

THE GUARDIANS OF THE SCROLL
The Vatican Vaults May 2000

This book is about how far man will go, to quench his insatiable greed, and his willingness to stop at nothing, in his hunt for the forbidden fruits of God's treasury, and about a certain piece of papyrus, found in May 2000, by a janitor, and given to a certain Vatican scholar, while working on the deciphering of certain documents in the Vatican catacombs, Father Vinchenzo, a priest and theologian, was working at the Vatican as a translator, while deciphering ancient Christian papyrus' that were kept in the vaults at the Vatican, with his small team of two others, Marcella, and Peter, he was given a small piece of papyrus that a janitor came across, in one of the vaults at the very back of a small room, this discovery was not unusual in-itself as many times this would occur in the many rooms, this was just another ordinary day at the office for Father Vinchenzo, and the team or so it would seem.

However, for Peter and Marcella what was about to be discovered, would be a life changing experience for both them, as they were unaware of who Father Vinchenzo really was even though they worked with him, the ramifications of what they were about to discover would lead them down a path that they would not easily forget for the rest of their lives.

The piece of papyrus they would decipher would lead them on a path of adventure, discovery, and danger, they as a team, would have to think and act quickly if they were to stay ahead of the game, there was no room for second chances, they would have to keep this discovery to themselves save a few chosen men in the priesthood.

This discovery would if followed through to the bitter end, eventually lead them to one of the most sorts after mysteries of God.

The expanse of this, will take the reader from the creation story of the Bible, through Roman occupied Palestine, The Third Reich, and to the present day, it will, if found, reveal death, hope, destruction, and disbelief into the lives of those who seek such treasures, these treasures are forbidden fruits, the type of treasure all men will crave after and kill for, yet were never meant to have, it will take the reader on a road to intrigue, cover up and denial, it will bring the religious authorities into question and leave people wondering just how much more they have subdued in their quest for power.

Some will say this book is fictional, yet others will wonder, just how true to life it is, others will be intrigued by its many facets of truth and deception, this book will be what people believe it to be, yet only the author will truly know whether what he reveals is true or not.

Some will say how could this be, yet others will say to themselves maybe this answers some of the unspoken questions that lie in the back of ones mind, never to be asked out loud, the danger that lies ahead will seem real to some people, yet ridicules to others, but the question here is, is it feasible?

Can this really be true, or is it just too far fetched? Well that is up to the reader to decide, not the author, as the author only writes what he imagines, not whether it is true or not, no, only God will know whether what he writes is fact or fiction.

This book is meant to challenge and perhaps excite the adventurer in each one of us, the names in this book are chosen at random, and should not characterize any particular person,

This story will lead us through the past, present and even at times, to the future and therefore, ultimately to the treasure sort, or maybe not who knows.

Man has sought over the centuries to discover the many treasures of this world, yet he is fast running out of things to discover, therefore he seeks for the ultimate treasures, that of the lost city of Atlantis, and the secret tombs of great kings, and pharaohs, and when he finds them he ransacks them of their many fine treasures, he displays them for all to see in most cases, yet in other cases hides them from others peoples view in the many private art collection all over the world.

Now what if there was a treasure so beautiful and expansive, that no one could take it, or display it, or for that matter hide it away in a private collection!

Suppose this treasure, had everything, man craved for, fore example a fountain of youth, the secret to eternal life, the secret of eternal health, riches beyond mans wildest dreams, just suppose you could find such a place, what would you do with it? Would you share it with others, or kill to protect its secrets!

We are all capable of killing if the price was right, we are all capable of greed taking hold of us, inside all of us is a monster waiting to get out, how far would you go, if pushed?

We live our lives not really knowing ourselves, we despise murder, rape, sodomy, liars, cheats, and yet we are all vulnerable to the attraction of all these things, we are all capable of doing such things, but our moral side stops us, and we live in society one with another, and no one really knows us, and what we are capable of deep down inside.

We judge others for what we ourselves are capable of, yet we show no compassion in theses matters, lets us therefore, stop and consider the consequences of such actions as deceit, murder, envy, pride, and greed, these are the five deadly sins, and they are in us all if we allow them to rule our lives, let us therefore, enter this world of intrigue, with open minds and see how much of ourselves we see in the adventure that lies ahead.

Let us first look at the background to this hidden treasure, that has eluded man since time began, this sought after treasure attracted the attention of kings, leaders, dictators, and men seeking power and riches beyond their wildest dreams.

In The Beginning the Garden Was Formed

Creations story! God created a wonderful garden here on earth and put man in it, there man named all the animals and the birds of the air, Genesis 2:19

*"Now the Lord God had formed out of the ground all
the beast of the field and the birds of the air.
He brought them to the man to see what he would name them; and
whatever the man called each living creature, that was its name."*
(N.I.V)

This garden was like none ever seen, or would ever be again, it was beautiful in every sense of the word, as recorded in the book of Genesis, in the books of the Bible and Torah, which are the Christian and Jewish books of the Old Testament.

Rocks filled with gold, and rubies as big as stones lay around, diamonds lit up the caves, there was the fountain of youth, the tree of life, and the tree of knowledge, where food was abundant and the treasures of the earth were to found in abundance, the garden is said to lead to a place where gold is in abundance, this land is called Pishon.

*"A river watering the garden flowed from Eden; from
there it separated into four headwaters.
The name of the first is Pishon; it winds through the
entire land of Havilah, where there is gold.
(The gold of that land is good; aromatic resin and onyx are also there),"*
(N.I.V)

The river that flows through the middle of the Garden of Eden is the river that also flows through the land of Havilah, this is the purest of gold is to be found, and the onyx stones that rival all others will be found.

This type of treasure has always attracted the greed of man; God knew this, so he hid the garden from man, when Adam and Eve, were thrown from the garden for their sin against God, Genesis 3:23-24

*"So the Lord God banished him (man) from the garden of
Eden to work the ground from which he had been taken.
After he drove man out, he placed on the east side of the garden
of Eden a cherubim (angel) and a flaming sword flashing
back and forth to guard the way to the tree of life."*
(N.I.V)

The garden was sealed from man and hidden out of sight, this garden if found would reveal all the secrets of the universe and of heaven itself, the power it would yield men would be overwhelming, the man who found it would rule the world once and for all, he would have unlimited power and resources, he would have unlimited wealth and health, he would seem unstoppable! Yet God knew his greed would be his downfall.

Just as the Ark of the covenant; that the Israelites had paraded before the congregation, as they went into battle was so powerful, that the enemy was thrown into confusion and disarray, so this discovery would make the Ark look like child's play if found.

We now have a basic idea as to the background to the Garden of Eden, how it evolved and why it is so sought after, so now let us begin the story of the lost Garden of Eden.

The chain of events will lead us through six millenniums, eight countries, ten cities, and numerous dead-ends.

CHAPTER 1
"Eden Project"
(The Secrets of the Papyrus)

It' was a beautiful summers day, as Father Vinchenzo left his apartment in Rome, he headed for the Vatican and the daily work, that lay before him, but he was not who he seemed to be, he lived a double life, he carried around with him a secret so great that only a few men could be trusted with it, men of honour, courage, and faith, he loved what he did, but he knew one day it would all have to end, but for now it was exciting deciphering all these unread parchments, often he would think to himself maybe! Just maybe, today will be the day that I come across a secret clue to a lost treasure, then he would smile to himself and think well that's enough fantasying for today, lets get on with the work in hand!

As he approached the door to the decipher room, Marcella, would meet him as usual in the corridor just before the entrance to the decipher room, they would politely pass the time of day, then enter the room to start the day ahead.

Peter, would greet them with a warm smile and a much needed cup of coffee, Marcella looked forward to this morning ritual, as it made him feel ready for the day ahead.

Peter, would then inform Father Vinchenzo, of his remit for that day, this usually included any new manuscripts to be deciphered, however, on this particular occasion Peter, had not mentioned any new assignments, this puzzled Father Vinchenzo, as Peter, was usually thorough in his duties, everyday for the last two years there was always a new list on Mondays, and as this was Monday morning there should have been a list.

Father Vinchenzo asked Peter, "If he had forgotten to mention anything?" Peter look puzzled at Father Vinchenzo, and replied "no I don't think so!"

Father Vinchenzo replied slightly baffled by this answer, "was there no list this morning?"

Peter suddenly realised why Father Vinchenzo had asked the questions Peter answered "oh sorry Father, no not this morning, the office computer that issued the lists had collapsed and was off line, due to a fault, I thought you knew, however they expect it to be up and running by tomorrow" Peter replied.

Father Vinchenzo just saying "that's alright Peter you weren't to know" he then smiled and left Peter to deal with the problems in hand. Meanwhile he would tie up the loose ends from the previous weeks work, he thought to himself for a moment, then what do I do, while I am waiting for the work load for the following week to begin?

Just then Angelo came in to the office, everyone looked surprised at this, because this had never happened before, Angelo, was one of the unsung hero's of the night staff, he and others like him came at midnight and left at dawn.

Father Vinchenzo asked "is there a problem Angelo?" Thinking something must be wrong! It had to be a problem of immense magnitude to bring Angelo in to see him, as this was the middle of the night for Angelo, Father Vinchenzo waited for Angelo to blurt out some sort of melodrama that had occurred during the night shift, however,

Angelo replied " there's no problem really, I just wanted to show you this piece of old parchment I found last night while cleaning out room 203, I thought you might like to view it before it is thrown away."

Father Vinchenzo, looked at Angelo, and said with a reassuring voice and a smile, "give it to Marcella, he will deal with it."

Angelo looked over to Marcella, who was at the photo copying machine, he turned and walked towards Marcella, with the piece of parchment in his hand.

"Marcella, Father Vinchenzo, asked me to give you this piece of parchment I found last night in room 203."

Marcella turned his head towards Angelo and beckoned him to put it on his desk, and then carried on with what he was doing.

It was about an hour later that Marcello was at a loose end, when he remembered the piece of parchment that Angelo had brought in to the office and offered it to him at the request of Father Vinchenzo, he picked it up, and carefully, unravelling it, he began to examining it when he noticed it had an uncanny familiarity to it, why! He was not sure but felt it needed closer examination it was like it was calling to him, he called over Father Vinchenzo, and Peter, and as all three looked at it, Father Vinchenzo noticed that Peter and Marcella had a look of uneasy excitement on their faces, Peter and Marcella were totally unaware of how they looked, they just knew they felt an uneasiness and yet excitement in their spirits, so Father Vinchenzo suggested that they begin to decipher as much of it as they could, it was then that Peter had remembered that two years previous to this find, a Father from Bonn in Germany, had been doing a study on the treasure hunt of the Third Reich, during the second world war, led by an Archaeologist by the name of Heinz Muller, which had gone desperately wrong!

Over fifty men had started the expedition to find what they called "The Papyrus of the Guardians of the Garden", this was supposedly a map that would lead them to a treasure so rich that no one man could own.

However, the work ceased because part of a document was missing and therefore, it was felt they could go no further.

This grabbed the attention of Marcella, as he knew in the early days Peter, had worked on this project, Peter was one of the team, working on the deciphering of the parchment in the expedition led by Father Kurt Barth, to try to find out, what happened to the fifty men on the original expedition in 1943.

He remembered, that the expedition was formed because of a letter found in early cuneiform writing to an ancient king of the Hittites in Canaan, named Ed-Baal who had sent a expedition force to seek out new lands in the far North, the letter came back after many seasons, saying, they had heard a rumour of a place were night never fell and the trees always produced fruit, it was a land of precious jewels and gold paved its streets nothing more was ever heard from that expedition.

3

Then in 1943 the Third Reich learnt of this the legend of this treasure and wanted to discover if this was true or not, so they set about researching all they could about this land.

Had it for instance been mentioned in any other communiqués throughout history, they turned up a further obscure mention of this place in a letter to Constantine Emperor of Rome from a Flavious Brutus a tribune in the Emperors guard who was instructed to inform the Emperor of an expedition that had been sent to investigate a rumour of a vast land filled with the treasures of a king call Soloma.

This could be translated as Solomon, however a later communiqué stated that 200 men had been lost on the expedition and therefore it was abandoned, there was no explanation as to why or how they were lost, just that they died doing their duty for the Emperor.

Father Vinchenzo, suggested they "begin to search for the missing file, so as to reunite the parchment to its correct place."

Father Vinchenzo then suggested "they say nothing about this discovery to anyone until he had all the relevant information at hand."

Marcella, decided to go into the archives and search for the missing "Kristos File" while Peter went to the records office of the Vatican to see if the file was there, Father Vinchenzo, meanwhile had to make sure Peter and Marcella, suspected nothing at this stage, so he would have to form an elaborate but believable excuse to be able to disappear for awhile.

He told Peter and Marcella "he would try to retrace the step of the commission led by Father Kurt, he would fly to Bonn, in Germany, to speak informally, with other members of the commission."

This after all he thought to himself, would not arouse any suspicion, as to why he was following this line of enquiry, as it was normal after a couple of years to follow up any enquiry just to make sure all the loose ends were taken care of, and he would use his good friend Father Angus Macintyre, as an excuse to visit Bonn, Father Angus, as he was known was a rather loud but lovable Scotsman, who chose to study and teach at Bonn University.

Vinchenzo informed Peter and Marcella of his intended opportunity to visit his old friend once again, he told them "he had fond memories of his time with Angus, during their training as priests."

Father Vinchenzo made the necessary plans for his journey, he booked a flight to Germany and made the necessary travel arrangements.

Father Vinchenzo, told them "he would stay with Angus his friend, and they would chat over old times and drink plenty of whisky as in the old days."

He told Peter and Marcella, "that the very thought of seeing Angus made him smile to himself, as he remembered at times; they got so drunk they never wanted to get out of bed again!"

"Well at least this time" he said, "they were much older and more mature now, so they would not drink so much! Hopefully that is."

Peter was speechless at the thought of Father Vinchenzo drunk, then he thought about how funny that could be, they all laughed at the thought of Father Vinchenzo, and Father Angus in a stupor.

Angus, always called him Vini for short, and always hugged him like a bear, Angus, was a big fellow, he told them, "with hands like shovels, and a laugh that thundered out, he had a red face and nose, in short he was the life and soul of the party."

The three men met back at the office the next morning, telling each other of their progress or lack of, whichever was the case.

Marcella seemed to have no trouble locating the file, so on his return they opened the file expecting to find the matching piece of the document, however, the file was intact except for that one piece of papyrus, which was defiantly missing.

They puzzled as to why, for it would seem to them it would be of no use to anyone else without the piece they had found.

Father Vinchenzo decided to look at the piece of papyrus again, but this time he would examine it under ultra violate light, this should show up things the human eye would miss.

He took the piece of papyrus to the lab, where he exposed it to controlled testing, as they watched closely, Peter, noticed something odd about the papyri, it seemed to glow, under the ultra violate light, this was not the norm at all.

Taking the papyrus from the light, and using a formulated liquid mixture, he lightly brushed the edges of the papyrus, the reaction on the edges told him this piece was not what it appeared, the reaction was all wrong, he took the piece of papyrus and exposed it to radiation, this would tell him the make up of the papyrus, it was obviously fake, but what hit them was why?, why was a fake piece of papyrus hidden in the vault of the Vatican, it could serve no purpose, no purpose at all? thought Peter, as did Marcello and Father Vinchenzo.

They returned to the office preoccupied with the thought of why?

Then suddenly Father Vinchenzo threw in a tit bit and said, "he remembered something he had read as a student some years ago, when he and Father Angus, had looked into the idea of, could the Garden of Eden still exist?"

But after further thought on the matter they decided this was probably ridiculous, and so they abandoned the whole idea!

Surely this has nothing to do with what they had found?

Nevertheless this penetrating thought nagged at Peter and Marcella all day, it was like they were being directed by someone or something towards this direction of thought.

Father Vinchenzo arrived home late that evening, he had set in motion the plans necessary for him to be able to manoeuvre into position his opportunity to leave without arousing unnecessary suspicion and by planting the thoughts into Peter and Marcella's minds as to why someone should leave a forge piece of papyrus in the vault, was pure genius so he went back to his office, as he entered the building he greeted the night porter said "good evening George!", George, was the night security guard.

George acknowledged him and said "are you working late tonight Father?"

Vinchenzo replied "yes unfortunately"

George replied "that's not like you Father".

"No!" Father Vinchenzo replied "just something I have to clear up before morning, guilty conscience I suppose" he said! George, smiled and nodded then went back to his book.

Father Vinchenzo had remembered at college he and Angus had used a solution of lemon and vinegar, to reveal a secret message on the back of a piece of papyrus, just for a laugh, Angus had got a fellow student to write a secret message on the back of the papyrus, and they had to retrieve it, as a part of an experiment they were carrying out.

Why this should come to him now he thought, only God knows, to most it would seem as though he was clutching at straws, but to Father Vinchenzo he had to be certain of what he thought was going on, he went to the lab with the piece of scroll, mixed up a solution of lemon and vinegar then carefully opening the scroll out he was about to begin to coat the back of the scroll with the solution, when suddenly the door opened, there stood Peter and Marcella, they asked "what are you was doing, Father Vinchenzo?" Vinchenzo sighed a breath of relief, he said "come in."

Marcella asked "are you alright Father?"

"Yes" explained Father Vinchenzo, "you startled me that's all."

He began to explain, that he could not settle and that all he could think of was the piece of scroll, and why anyone would plant a forged piece of papyrus in an empty vault in the Vatican.

Peter replied "they too could not settle for that very reason and felt led to come to the office, it was as if something was drawing them to the come here!"

Marcella remarked "that for some reason he felt there could be something written on the back of the parchment", just as Father Vinchenzo had for some reason remembered that experiment from his college days, Marcella, also felt there might be something on the back of the piece of parchment.

Father Vinchenzo returned to the experiment, he began to brush the solution over the back of the piece parchment and then waited for a reaction, their wait was short lived, a series of figures appeared, they ran from left to right which was unusual as normally they would run from right to left, then in a small corner the name Father K Barth, and the words "I have found Heinz Muller's expedition God help us now!"

This was indeed a shock to them all, as Vinchenzo was under the impression that Father Kurt as he was known, had passed away peacefully in his bed in Düsseldorf but according to this he passed away alright! But far from peacefully, as underneath these words where written, Kristos expedition, this expedition had been abandoned because the main part of the team had vanished without trace.

This puzzled Vinchenzo, as he was led to believe Father Kurt, had retired to his home in Düsseldorf, because of ill health and passed away peacefully in his sleep.

At the time Vinchenzo, thought nothing of this as Father Kurt was an older man, "but not frail", he told the others!

This was all an elaborate plan, to keep Peter and Marcella keen.

He continued to say, "now I come to think of it he seemed healthy enough to me! but then, illness can strike us all at a moments notice" then he said "still there was the question nagging away at him, why should this piece of papyrus end up in the vaults in the Vatican, and even more important why should it arrive at our place of work?" These questions would remain with them for a while yet, before they would finally piece together the pieces of the puzzle that lay before them, tantalisingly, eating at Peter and Marcella's inquisitive nature, they most certainly had that! thought Vinchenzo, perhaps that's why they were sent to him, perhaps they were meant to arrive in his office in some sort of supernatural way.

Was it a divine intervention that led Angelo to bring this piece of papyrus into his office? was I supposed to unravel yet another attempt on this divine hidden secret he thought to himself? Then he thought, boy this was turning out to be a week to remember!.

The next morning, Vinchenzo, Peter, and Marcella were sitting at a table outside the "Café Dantino's" in the square, they often met here for coffee during morning break they would discuss the work a head and plan how they would tackle it, so for them to meet here was not out of place, in-fact quite the opposite, it would seem as all was normal, they were deliberating over the dilemma they were in, who could they tell, who would listen without thinking they were out of their minds, overcome by intrigue, and the wildness of their imagination, Vinchenzo warned them, "say nothing to anyone, they must first establish the facts and find out if any of this is true, or if this was deliberately planted to test their devotion to the everyday tasks, to see if they are truly committed!" Vinchenzo' thoughts began to deepen, may be this was a ploy to smoke him out into the open for who he really was?

It was getting to close for comfort for Vinchenzo, however, the men agreed they would discretely work on this project, in their own time, they agreed to meet at Vinchenzo' house after work and continue to work on the project each evening, this would avert any un-necessary attention being directed towards them.

The next day all at the office continued as normal, the relevant documents were catalogued and work began on schedule to decipher them, this was what was expected by their superiors.

At the end of each working day they would meet at Vinchenzo' as agreed, and begin work on finding out what these numbers meant, this was a great puzzle to them. Vinchenzo suggested to Peter "that he should once again fetch the piece of parchment so they may examine the back of it again."

Vinchenzo was not sure why he had requested this, as this would draw Peter and Marcella into the spiders web and therefore greater danger, however this he felt had to be done.

Peter, brought the piece of papyrus to Vinchenzo, Vinchenzo, opened the piece of papyrus and turned it over on the back there were only numbers and the small inscription, may be he thought to himself, there might be something they had missed?

Peter, was now examining the discoloured piece of papyrus which he had brought to Vinchenzo, as he laid it on the table he noticed a small mark in the corner near the top number and two small vertical lines next to each of the other numbers, he pointed this out to Vinchenzo who immediately looked up, saying "where did they come from?"

Marcella suggested, "that an explanation for not having seen them before, was that they must have appeared after they had examined the partial piece of parchment, this would make sense of why they had never noticed these markings before!"

Vinchenzo looked at Marcella, then at Peter and said "that must be it, there's no other possible explanation", all agreed, and began to try to find out what these markings meant.

Peter, remembered from way back in his early days as a child he would go sailing with his grandfather, he remembered the night before they would go sailing, that his grandfather would plot the course they were to take while sailing, then his grandfather would give it to the coast guard the next day just before they went sailing, his grandfather would say it was in case anything went wrong they would know where to start looking.

Peter said "these marks looked like the sort you found on charts."

Vinchenzo suggested "that the next day at lunchtime, Peter should go to the library and see if they held any charts or similar documents that may help then to decipher the numbers on the back of the piece of papyrus".

They agreed this would be the next course of action, and decided they had done enough for today and they would résumé in the morning at coffee outside the Café.

After the men left Vinchenzo, sat in a large armchair near the fire mulling over the events of the last few days in his mind, he wasn't sure how far the implications of this problem would lead them, he thought he should contact the other guardians and inform them of the situation so far, as things were moving fast and could get out of hand at any moment if one was not careful better safe than sorry eh!

The next morning Peter and Marcella, were waiting for Father Vinchenzo outside the Café at break time as usual, however this morning he seemed rather later than usual, this they would find out was due to Monsignor Gazelle, who was head of the department, having called Vinchenzo in to ask him about the progress of his office on the deciphering of certain texts that had been forwarded to his office, this of course was a regular occurrence that need not worry anyone normally, however, in this case Father Vinchenzo was rather taken back by some of the Monsignor' remarks, there was something about this meeting that gave him an uncomfortable feeling, he couldn't put his finger on it, but there was something? he thought.

He met Peter and Marcella at the Café, he was running later and told them "he would speak to them later explaining all that went on in the meeting".

He hurriedly drank his coffee, leaving Peter, and Marcella feeling quite breathless, then dashed off.

Marcella said to Peter: "I wonder what all that was about."

Peter just shrugged his shoulders and said "we'll find out later I am sure."

Father Vinchenzo was out all day, neither, Peter nor Marcella knew where he was, this was quite worrying as whenever he would be out of the office he always left a contact number or address where he could be reach in emergencies.

Peter, reassured Marcella saying "don't worry he will be alright he is a resourceful chap and capable of looking after himself, besides, Peter said, we will find out more tonight."

Six o'clock they all met at Father Vinchenzo', Father Vinchenzo had already put the kettle on for a cup of coffee, this would help them to settle ready for them to begin, Marcella straightaway asked "are you alright Father Vinchenzo, we were worried where were you?"

Peter said "hush Marcella, give Father Vinchenzo time to tell us, first have your cup of tea."

Father Vinchenzo said, "no that's alright Peter, Marcella has a right to know, as do you where I have been all day and why."

He began by saying to them, "as you know every month I am called to Monsignor Gazelle to give an update on the work in hand, as he is the oversight on the deciphering project."

He began to tell them what had happened, when he had visited Monsignor Gazelle, "the meeting began as usual with the niceties and then the progress report, however, this quickly changed to Monsignor Gazelle, asking me if we had received any unusual pieces of documentation, I of course replied someone had passed onto us a small piece of papyrus, which was of no use, as we recognised it to be a forgery, this was revealed through certain tests we had done on the paper, the carbon 14 dating had revealed it to be less than 5 years old, so we put it in an envelope and sent it to the achieves, as is procedure in these cases."

Then Monsignor Gazelle, went on to say "are you sure it was valueless?"

"I just shrugged my shoulders and said yes I thought so, he laughed and said good bye, but I felt there was more to this than met the eye, he seemed to know more than he was willing to say, we must be careful and if anyone else comes around asking questions direct them to me."

Peter and Marcella agreed, they then began to look at the papyrus once more, Peter had managed to obtain a chart and a book on circum navigation, without too much difficulty, he began to look up the chart longitudes and latitudes, and cross referencing them with the numbers on the back of the papyrus, but it made no sense at first, the numbers did not mach up, they stood and thought, but still it made no sense except for one number, this was 66 degrees, this was of course true north on the chart, but this figure was smack centre of the line of figures, then Father Vinchenzo suggested "that they should work all calculations out from this point" they all agreed and began the work.

They toiled all evening to no avail, Father Vinchenzo, was starting to feel perhaps its time to give up and accept these are not map reference points.

Peter, and Marcella, too were beginning to doubt the validity of these being map reference points, then in a flash Peter remembered "that his grandfather had played a game with him while they were on the Yacht, he used to set out a course for home, but ask Peter to plot the course on the chart with the reference points his grandfather had given him, the catch was, the reference points where in reverse order, this made the challenge a bit harder, what if these reference points were reversed?"

Peter suggested, "that maybe these were in reverse order too!"

Vinchenzo and Marcella, just looked at each other, Marcella said "but surely that's too easy!"

Father Vinchenzo remarked "yes so easy we missed it, we've tried every way but this way what have we to lose, right Father Vinchenzo said, let's give it ago! The easy ways are the most over looked ways in my opinion."

They began to reverse the order of the numbers; the only number irreversible was true north, so they accepted this was either the starting point or the directional point, so this was to be left alone.

They became aware that all of these degrees in reverse represented a location on the world map, each location was a country or city, these covered the world; from the North Pole to the Antarctica, from South America to Africa, but why?

This question beckoned an answer, to try to find it would be dangerous and difficult, however, this must be sought.

Father Vinchenzo asked Peter "to search out discreetly the file on the "Eden Project"." This was a file on an expedition in 125A.D, led by Festus Brutus, a tribune in the Emperors personal guard, in which they had found evidence to suggest that a garden full of mystical things and treasures, guarded by an unseen protector actually existed. The information had come to them via stories which had been passed down by Bedouin traders, who had passed by on several occasions in Egypt near to the Pharaohs place between 1090B.C 1000 B.C this had been recorded by the Pharaohs of that dynasties of Thotmes III and his successor Amenophis IV, his wife was Nefertiti, in this letter it had mentioned that Pharaoh had sent several unsuccessful expeditions out to look for this lost garden, but alas none had returned.

Father Vinchenzo then turned to Marcella and said, "Marcella you go to room 407 and look out a file named 'The Pentateuch Project' this was a list of all stories told about unusual myths or legends that had been spoken about in the times of the Old Testament period between Abraham and the coming of John the Baptist."

Marcella nodded, and said "ok I have a friend there we can trust who will help us." Father Vinchenzo quickly replied "no friends! not at this stage at least! as it is too dangerous we need to find out who is worthy of our trust as all are possible spies for the Monsignor at the moment."

They all finally agreed and felt at this time things should stay in the family as it were.

They agreed to meet the next day at the Café to make plans for that coming evening, as they would decide the best course of action to go forward in.

Vinchenzo felt it was time to contact the others, and make his supposed plans to go and see Father Angus in Germany, there was too much going on here and he was sworn to protect the secret he held but things, were getting to out of hand to be certain of keeping the secret safe, he needed help and he needed it now! He thought to himself, the next day they met as agreed on the previous evening.

On the way to the Café Father Vinchenzo, noticed a black coloured car sitting just around the corner from the Café the men in it seemed familiar so he went over to it to invite them to have coffee with him and the others.

As Vinchenzo, approached the car he noticed the men duck down, he stopped! and realised who these men were, they were aids to Monsignor Gazelle, he tried to act natural and passed them the men in the car, as he approached the café Peter and Marcella, turned to greet him, but he lightly shook his head and walked on by Peter and Marcella realised something was wrong they waited a few minutes, then finished their coffee acting as natural as possible in the process.

Peter said to Marcella "well it's time to start work, I suppose we had better go", Peter said this in as loud a voice as was appropriate but without trying to arouse suspicion.

Marcella agreed, and both men rose and headed in the direction of the Vatican vaults, they arrived in the office and asked what was happening? Vinchenzo held his finger to his lips, motioning silence, he wrote on a piece of paper, don't talk, place bugged, we will meet at my place at six!

Peter and Marcella nodded and started the days work that lay ahead of them, the day seemed to drag for Marcella, as he was anxious to know what was going on, six o'clock came and as Peter and Marcella, approached Father Vinchenzo' flat, they noticed a dark coloured vehicle in the street opposite Father Vinchenzo', Peter motioned Marcella to wait, he took out his mobile and called Father Vinchenzo. Vinchenzo picked up the phone answering it "hello Father Vinchenzo speaking."

Peter began to explain where they where and why they were late, Peter told him to "look out of his window and see if he could see the vehicle on the corner?"

Vinchenzo said "no! he couldn't!"

They decided it was safe for them to come up via the rear entrance, as the men in the car were unable to see the rear entrance from where they were situated, Peter and Marcella, slipped in the back way of the building, un-noticed by the men in the vehicle outside, they entered by the rear door, up the fire escape and into Father Vinchenzo' flat.

Marcella was worried "that so much had happened in such a short space of time!" Father Vinchenzo agreed, as did Peter, Father Vinchenzo informed them "that he had decided it was time for him to take a sabbatical, and visit Father Angus in Bonn, he would make the arrangements to leave on Friday, he would inform the Monsignor of his intent first thing in the morning". Peter said "was this wise, in the light of what had happened since his last meeting with the Monsignor?" Father Vinchenzo stopped and thought for a moment, he paused, saying "yes perhaps you're right Peter!", Peter, "you will have to cover for me, if they ask where I am make up some excuse, that should give me a couple of days, even with all this attention I am receiving."

Peter agreed, as did Marcella, Father Vinchenzo carefully looked out of his window to see if the coast was clear, however, in the shadow of a doorway he could just make out the silhouette of a what could be a man, so Peter and Marcella left the same way they came in through the back of the building.

They had arrange to meet up as usual at the cafe as to avert any suspicion, by not changing their daily routine, they would make everyone think all was ok, that they suspected nothing and had not realised they were being watched.

The next day as usual the three met at the café, they had their coffee, speaking only about that, day's projects, which lay ahead of them, they finished their discussion and headed for the office.

They arrived in the office ready to start work, Father Vinchenzo sorted out with the relevant documentation for that day passing it on to Peter and Marcella for processing into the necessary files.

As the day drew on Father Vinchenzo had to make his mid week trip to the airport to collect any further material found at the digs in Mesopotamia which would need cataloguing and processing, this gave him a window of opportunity to buy the airline tickets, to Bonn, therefore averting any reason for anyone to suspect anything was wrong.

This was the opportunity he was waiting for, the car would pick him up at two o-clock sharp, he would be able to slip in and get the tickets while waiting for customs to release the artefacts to him, this would allow Monsignor Gazette's henchmen time to observe him buying the tickets, then he would be back in the office at three thirty he thought to himself.

The time came to leave for the airport, and as usual the driver arrived right on time. They returned at precisely three thirty as expected and no one suspected anything, Father Vinchenzo was pleased with himself, he thought "he liked this cloak and dagger stuff" to himself, he loved the sense of adventure that came with the job as an intrepid explorer, hiding in the shadows waiting for his next adventure to start, then he thought to himself well may be, but there's a lot to think about and dangers to be overcome, and returned to the reality of the job in hand.

Friday morning came, Father Vinchenzo woke early, he had packed his bag that previous evening, he got up had shower, and dressed quickly, time was of the essence here he thought to himself, everything had been meticulously planned, Peter would arrive at the office at precisely nine thirty, were Marcella would inform him I had gone to a village on the outskirts of Rome to see a local priest on a matter of urgency, and would be out of the office all day.

By this time he would be safely on the plane, heading for Bonn, provided all went to plan.

Father Vinchenzo, of course; could not leave through the front so he had told the taxi to pick him up at the rear entrance, his flight was due to leave at eight forty five, therefore, he must leave soon to check in and buy a magazine for the flight.

He left by the backdoor and went to the airport arriving there just as check in was called, he headed for the departure gate and handing his boarding pass to the gate attendant he boarded the flight with out difficulty, he actually smiled to himself as to how easy this had been, however he knew in reality this was a dangerous mission he was on.

He was to phone the office and they were to wait before answering it, if the phone went dead after three rings, they would know he was safely on his way to Bonn, or so they would think to Father Angus' in Bonn.

Father Vinchenzo picked up his phone and began to ring the number, it rang three times and then he hung up quickly.

Peter was in the office, the phone rang he waited paused to pick it up, he listened for the fourth ring, the phone stopped at the third ring, he sighed with relief when it stopped, he smiled to himself and continued with his work.

When Marcella returned, he looked at Peter, Peter just smiled reassuringly and Marcella felt that same sigh of relief within himself, at the thought of everything going to schedule.

That day seemed to take for ever, at the close of the day Peter and Marcella decided they would go for a drink after work, just to celebrate the fact that Father Vinchenzo was safely on his way.

They left the office and went to Dominos bar, near to where they worked it was a place where most of the staff at the Vatican would gather at the end of the working day, they chose this as it seemed it would be he safest place to go for a quick drink before going home together.

Marcella was afraid that the men watching Father Vinchenzo' flat may try to cause problems, Peter, thought Marcella was over dramatising the situation but would go along with the idea.

It was about eight thirty when they left the bar in the Plaza, they turned west and headed for home, Marcella noticed a car which seemed to be following them at a discrete distance, Marcella mentioned this to Peter, who looked back but saw nothing. Peter said, "don't be silly Marcella, there is nothing there."

Marcella replied "I'm sure I saw a car, it was there honestly!"

They entered the street were they lived, and headed towards the house when suddenly two men in over coats came out of the shadows, Peter shouted to Marcella "run! run for it", but they were too late, a car came screeching around the corner pulled up sharply and they were bundled into the car, a blanket was thrown over them then Peter felt a sharp pain in the back of his neck, he felt himself going faint then nothing, Marcella, felt Peter keel over onto him, he shuddered with fear, "what was to become of them? Marcella wondered!"

Marcella thought Peter had been shot or something, then a cold shiver came over him, was he next he thought, he felt a warm sensation in his arm, as he realised they had injected him with something he was aware that he was tired, O' so tired, then he felt his eyes shut.

The next thing either one of them knew was the sound of bells ringing in their ears, loud bells! Peter opened his eyes, and saw Marcella laying their motionless, he shook Marcella, Marcella opened one eye, and looking at Peter he gingerly said, "are we dead?"

Peter smiled at Marcella, he replied "no Marcella we are not dead yet!", Peter looked around the room, there wasn't much to see the window was boarded up and the only light came from the cracks in the wood and a candle in the middle of a little table that stood in the middle of the floor, two dishes, with what looked like, some bread and cheese in them stood either side of the candle, the cheese looked mouldy, yet edible to a hungry man but they were not that hungry yet, Peter thought to himself.

Just then Marcella sat up, "what has happened?" he said as he held his head.

Peter replied "we've been kidnapped I think!"

Marcella looked at Peter, "kidnapped! Kidnapped, why should anyone want to kidnap me, anyway isn't that illegal, he said?"

Peter replied "I don't know why we have been kidnapped, but I suspect it's to do with the piece of papyrus we were given, but I do intend to find out the truth as to why!"

Just then; Peter heard voices coming towards the room, Peter and Marcella, stood there bated breath, as the key turned in the lock,

Marcella grabbed Peters hand, they looked at each other, they could see the fear in each others eyes as the door handle turned, the door opened very gently at first, then flung back, Peter and Marcella' hands squeezed tighter, two huge figures stood silhouetted in the light there seemed an endless silence, then Peter cried out "who are you?"

The figures just laughed then shut the door locking it behind them, Peter and Marcella slumped to the floor exhaustion and fear, Marcella began to cry and said "we're going to die aren't we!"

Peter put his arm around Marcella's shoulder and squeezed, "not if I can help it he said."

Marcella just slumped into Peter's arms sobbing, and said "I don't want to die."

It was some time later when Marcella woke, Peter was doing something near the window, Marcella rubbed his eyes and looked again, Peter turned and looked at Marcella, "don't worry he said I'll soon have us out of here."

Marcella rose to his feet and went over to Peter, Peter, had taken a piece of wood from the broken window and began to scrape at the wall he found the wall was damp and flaky this was a weak point, so he had kept on digging and was almost through, the hole was just big enough for a small hand to reach through and shake the wooden panel that covered the window, this might just shake loose and allow them to attempt an escape Peter thought to himself.

Suddenly the voices drew near once more, Peter stopped gouging at the wall with the wood, the key once again turned in the lock the door swung open to reveal a slender figured gentleman dress in an SS officers uniform, of the "Third Reich", he entered the room followed by the two stocky gentlemen, he paused for a moment then asked Peter, "where Father Vinchenzo was?"

Peter replied "I have no idea."

The men laughed, then one of the larger men took hold of Marcella drew his gun from its holster and he put it to Marcella' head, the man repeated, "where is Father Vinchenzo?"

Peter paused and thought for a moment, Father Vinchenzo would want me to answer, saving Marcella's life, but what if I do tell them were Father Vinchenzo is? They may still shoot Marcella, then he thought, but if I don't tell them they will shoot Marcella anyway I'm sure of it!

Marcella was whimpering like a little puppy, he was terrified, the man asked again "where is Father Vinchenzo?"

Peter replied "let Marcella go and I will tell you."

The man nodded to the other man and he let go of Marcella, Marcella, fell to the ground in a heap as if all his energy had left him in one massive movement, just as Peter started to speak, a commotion was heard in the back ground, a forth person appeared, lent forward to the mans ear and whispered something, whatever it was, it must have been urgent, for suddenly the men left the room, locking the door behind them.

The commotion drew closer and closer, they could hear, what sounded like gun fire, Peter suddenly shouted to Marcella "get down!", there was a loud bang and the door flew open, two men grabbed them and standing them on their feet said, "quickly follow us."

Peter and Marcella didn't question the request, they just followed, there were dead bodies all over the place including the men who had threatened Marcella and Peter, they were led to an awaiting lorry were several what looked like soldiers were waiting, they got in the back of the lorry, then the lorry and the soldiers left with them on board.

As they travelled Peter thanked the men for their rescue but no one spoke it was like they were not there, after some while they entered what looked like an airfield, at the end of the concrete stood a large grey building, it looked like a hanger of some kind, the lorry entered it and they were told to get out.

They were led to a small room where they were told to stay until someone came for them, after several minutes a man entered the room with an English accent, he asked "if they were alright?"

Peter answered "yes thank you, but who are you? and what the hell is happening to us?"

The man reassured Peter and said "all he could say was they were taking them to England."

Peter stood for a moment, he felt numb from the statement he had just heard, then replied "why the hell do I want to go to England! for gods sake?"

The man smiled reassuringly and said "you'll find out all in good time."

Just then a man entered the room informing the officer that the plane had landed, "thank you" he said, the man looked at Peter and said "look we need to move fast on this, as we are not really supposed to be here if you know what I mean, so please no more questions for the time being, follow me as quickly as possible."

Peter and Marcella just looked at each other in bewilderment, but agreed and followed the man out to the airstrip where the plain lay in wait.

They boarded the plain and took off immediately to the sound of gun fire, this was not a good day thought Peter, firstly Father Vinchenzo leaves for Bonn, then they are kidnapped, and now they are on a plain for god knows where, and being shot at in the process, then he thought to himself, but we are still alive thank God!

Marcella was still shaking from the effects of the events that had taken place, he just sat there, in shock, the flight, seemed to take ages then without warning the officer in charge told them to fasten their seat belts, the plain shuddered as if someone or something had grabbed hold of it and shook it in mid air.

Peter and Marcella squeezed each others hand, suddenly a loud bang rung in their ears it sounded like the wings of the plain had departed from the fuselage, there was a sudden jerk, everyone seemed to lurch forward and the plane came to a sudden halt, everyone rose quickly from their seats, the doors were flung open and everyone ordered to leave the plain as quickly as possible.

Peter noticed smoke coming from the direction of the cockpit he quickly got up dragging poor Marcella with him and headed for the nearest exit, by this time Marcella was alert once again, as they reach the exit two men helped them out of the plane, they had landed safely on the tarmac.

Peter and Marcella looked back at the aircraft, it was full of bullet holes, the cockpit seemed to be the worst hit area, then two men emerged from the forward exit carrying a stretcher, two more men followed in what seemed quick succession with another stretcher.

Peter asked the officer what was going on? he replied "we were in a bit of a fix, the cockpit took most of the flack, however the pilot got us back, he and the co-pilot bought it I'm afraid, good men too, but at least they got us down safely before they died!"

Peter stood for a moment speechless, words where at a loss, "why had these men risked their lives for us?, why them?, who are they? And most of all who do they work for?"

They left the airfield, and drove for about an hour before they came to a large house in the country, there seemed to be nothing else around for miles, the two men were told to wait in a large room, the officer called it the reception.

After a short while the door opened and in walked Father Vinchenzo, Peter and Marcella were shocked yet so pleased to see he was ok that they totally forgot what they had gone through for a split second, the three men hugged each other and sat down on the sofa which was near a great big fire place, Peter had so many questions, as did Marcella, but Father Vinchenzo, told them to rest from their ordeal first then all their questions would be answered in time he promised them.

The two men were shown to their rooms, they where huge, Peter saw the bed and fell on it exhausted, as did Marcella, the two men were safe now, thank God they thought.

Peter, thought to himself I'm glad Father Vinchenzo was safe, but shouldn't he be in Germany, visiting Father Angus?, Peter, was exhausted and thought to himself, this is no time for such questions this is time to rest, all these questions can be asked later,

Peter woke up after what seemed a mere moment in time, he got up and had a shower, then dressed, he went to the window and opened it, it looked out over the beautiful countryside, he thought to himself had this all been a dream!

Then the bedroom door opened, there stood Father Vinchenzo, smiling as usual, "good afternoon Peter he said."

Peter replied "is it really? Have I slept that long, I thought a good nights rest would be enough, with all the questions I have, is Marcella up yet?"

"no! Father Vinchenzo replied, he's still sleeping! well lets go and have afternoon tea shall we."

"Fine" replied Peter, "and then you can tell me what this is all about."

Father Vinchenzo smiled and the two men left the room to go down stairs to the sitting room, moments later Marcella arrived refreshed after his rest, the three men sat around a lavish coffee table, Vinchenzo pulled on a long chord, a few moments later the door to the room opened and in came an elderly gentleman carrying a tray with cakes, a teapot, and cups and saucers on it, he put them down on the coffee table, then asked Vinchenzo "if there was anything else they required?"

Vinchenzo replied "no that will be all Jenkins."

Jenkins replied "very good milord", and left the room, Peter look astonished m'lord where did that come from he thought, Vinchenzo looked at him, and began to explain that he was not really who they thought he was yes he was Father Vinchenzo and a priest, but he was a special type of priest, one known more commonly as a "Guardian of the Scroll" as were the men who rescued them.

Peter looked puzzled as did Marcella, Peter replied "they are just legends, stories told to the young priest, "Guardians of the Scroll" he said abruptly."

Vinchenzo looked him square in the eye, sit down Peter and Marcella and listen to what I have to say and pay close attention I implore you, he began to tell them all about the scroll and what it meant, he then explained the mission that lay ahead, then he told them that "if they wanted to quit and go home they would understand", but also pointed out that should they take this course of action they could not guarantee their safety as they would be targets from now on in for the ruthless men they had just been liberated from.

Peter thought for a moment, thinking if they go home there may be others waiting for them, just to torture and kill them; if they stay and go on this mission they may probably die anyway! Peter thought long and hard before he looked at Vinchenzo, he said, "what option is there for us, if we don't go we will probably die if we do go we will probably die, is that really a choice, so I think we have a better chance with you than without you! I'm in."

Marcella, asked "will I have to use a gun?"

Vinchenzo replied, "not if you don't want to."

Marcella said "good then I'm in."

They agreed to see it though to the bitter end and they hugged each other once again. Peter suddenly thought to himself, hold on one moment! what is the mission? He asked Vinchenzo "what is the mission was?"

But Vinchenzo, said "patience Peter, all in good time, all in good time! First enjoy the rest, and then we'll talk!"

CHAPTER 2
The Journey

Peter and Marcella had been at the country Mansion for over a week now, they were getting impatient at the length of time they had to wait, they decided to go and ask Father Vinchenzo how much longer they would have to wait before they were told what this was all about.

They arrived at Father Vinchenzo' study, Peter knocked at the door of the study, a voice beckoned them in, it was Father Vinchenzo' voice, they entered the room to find several oddly dressed people in the room with him.

Peter apologised for the intrusion saying "sorry Father we didn't know you had company, we'll come back later."

Vinchenzo said, "That's alright Peter I was just about to send for you both any way."

He began to introduce Peter and Marcella to the others, this gentlemen is the two I told you about, "Hindrich, Gustava, Abdul, Franz, John, Michael, Ivan, this is Peter, and Marcella, say hello."

They all welcomed them into the presence, then Vinchenzo began with the story of "how he and these other gentlemen were the "Guardians of the Sacred Scrolls", the "Sacred Scrolls" were the legendary maps that led to the "Sacred Treasures of God!" the "Garden of Eden" being one of them, which had been entrusted to Godly men over the centuries, they had seen many men fight over the scrolls, and die trying to get them."

"However" Vinchenzo continued, in 1942 the Germans had come into possession of this particular map, they had found it in Egypt, in the upper Nile region, near the famed city of Memphis, but its potential had not then been recognised fully at the time of its discovery, and lay in a tomb for some time along with other relics waiting to be shipped back to Berlin for a more thorough analysis."

Again Vinchenzo continued with, "the artefacts never left Egypt, so they sent an archaeologist to verify the finds and to catalogue them.

This archaeologist was a Heinz Muller, who found the scroll amongst some other pieces of papyrus that he had been examining, he immediately recognised it to be of great value in the world of antiquities, he rolled up the scroll and smuggled it out of Egypt just before the allied invasion in 1945, it was told that Hitler had ordered Muller to take an expedition to find this great treasure, but once again this was a disaster the expedition never returned all were lost, and never heard of again."

Vinchenzo continued "then it disappeared for some twenty years before it turned up again in Munich, in 1965, it appeared on the black market it was sold to a Mr P Getti, who was a renown collector of fine art and artefacts he kept it under lock and key until his house was ransacked on his death, most people suspected his secretary, but this could never be proven, as Hinckley was found dead some weeks later, they said he hung himself because of his guilty conscience, this was in 1968."

He said "in 1969 it appeared again in South America, where it stayed until 1970 in a private collection, the scroll then disappeared again in 1971 from, Rio De Janeiro, they say a Nazi movement got hold of it the whole group disappeared save one man who came out of the jungle in a state of mental collapse, he was questioned but was unable to answer any of the questions put to him."

"Where is he now!" Asked Peter?

Vinchenzo replied "no one knows! Some say the fellow killed himself a year after he was found, but that was never certain as no one could prove this fact, however, when he was found all he went on about was devils and monsters with flashing blades of fiery steel."

Peter looked at Marcella; he was glued to the parchment fragment absorbed in the story and the piece of parchment, as if nothing else mattered but this moment in time, Peter smiled to himself, then turned and again listening intently to what Vinchenzo was saying.

Father Vinchenzo went on to say, "that the scroll had stayed buried until 1996 when it was once again discovered in a private art collection, which was sent for cleaning, the scroll was hidden inside one of the treasures, it was found by a young archaeological student working in a restoration department in the British Museum during his semesters, he took it home and there studied the scroll, he and a few of his friends decided they would try to locate the "Garden" as a project for their third year exams this was unwittingly agreed by their year tutor, they set off in the Autumn of 96, but never returned, search parties were sent out but to no avail, it was like they disappeared from the face of the earth!"

However, Vinchenzo, started to say, "We do have one advantage this time, over all the other times."

"And what's that?" Marcella asked rather shyly.

Vinchenzo brought out a note book, "this is Daniel Browns note book in which he wrote down his planned route."

"Hang on a moment" Peter said, "are you not the guardians of the scroll? can't you just go to where the "Garden" is located and see if they arrived there or not?"

Vinchenzo smiled, "no! Peter" he said, "we are only the "Guardians of the Scroll, not the keepers of the gate, we know where the "Garden" is located, and can if allowed go to the entrance of the "Garden" however, we can never enter it in earthly terms, for us it is enough to know the location and guarded the map."

Peter looked surprised at this statement! what did Vinchenzo mean by this so he asked, Vinchenzo, "so why are we here then and who were those men who kidnapped us?"

Vinchenzo began with the men who had kidnapped them, he told them "they were Nazi's, still trying to get hold of the map for themselves, they wanted to use the treasure to finance a new uprising of Aryanism, and to wipe out the Jews who they see as defilers of the sacred name of God, to systematically cleanse the world of impure blood, to destroy all Semitic tribes from the face of the earth, they were bigoted fanatics whose soul purpose was to inflict pain and misery where ever they could!."

Vinchenzo seemed passionate on this subject, so Peter quickly changed the subject

And said, "but that does not explain why we are here?"

Vinchenzo started to speak, then Ivan, who had not said much up to this point, interrupted with, "Father Vinchenzo allow me to answer that question", Vinchenzo nodded his approval.

Ivan began to explain the importance of retrieving the map, "the map had always been in the possession of the "Guardians" since the time Adam and Eve had been cast from the "Garden", God had placed a guardian at the entrance to the garden he was to defend the entrance with his life and a sword of fire was his weapon he was to let no man pass."

Peter replied, "Well if no man can pass then these guys, if they found it would be dead therefore, it would seem to me to be pointless going after them?"

Ivan looked at Peter and smiled, "that would be true except for one thing, and that is Brown still could be in possession of the map, and if that is the case, we need to retrieve it."

Peter looked up sheepishly and nodded his approval, Marcella, looked at Peter, and said "I'm glad you asked that question because I was beginning to ask myself the same questions", Peter smiled and apologised to Ivan, Ivan looked up and said in a gentle voice "never apologise for asking the obvious, someone has to", Peter, felt a lot better after that comment.

Vinchenzo called an end to the meeting and suggested they reconvene in the morning where they could continue to discuss the way ahead and answer any more questions Peter or Marcella may have for them, the men all agreed this was probably a good time to break for the evening, just then the old man reappeared, "dinner is served milord."

"Thank you Jenkins", replied Vinchenzo, "shall we gentlemen" as he pointed to the door, Jenkins, turned and left the room the other men began to follow, they entered the large dinning room where the table was set, the men took their places and the meal arrived, they began with Brown Windsor soup then they were served with pheasant, and venison pie, new potatoes, and a variety of good wholesome vegetables followed by Pavlova, Peter had, had eaten this English cuisine before, but for Marcella, this was his first time, he had rarely eaten outside of

Italy, he had once or twice tasted French cuisine, but that was it and he wasn't over keen on that it was too greasy for his delicate pallet this could be a problem Peter thought.

Marcella looked at Peter, Peter looked back at him reassuringly, saying "its ok Marcella the food is excellent."

Marcella smiled and began to eat the meal laid before him, the wine was a claret, a rather fine one at that, Marcella liked the wine however, as Peter suspected the meal was a tad forceful for him, but he enjoyed the vegetables very much.

After dinner the men retired to the drawing room for brandy and cigars, Marcella asked Peter "why they were there after all he didn't smoke and brandy always made him feel sick, just the smell of it was enough to make him head for the toilet?"

Peter said reassuringly "the English always do this, it's a kind of tradition to have a night cap before retiring for the night."

Marcella thought to himself, this is an odd custom, but acceptable I suppose after all he was in a foreign country, Peter suggested to Marcella, that they should retire to bed, leaving Vinchenzo, and the others to catch up on old times, as they seemed to have a lot to talk about, Marcella agreed, Peter coughed in a gentle way, Vinchenzo looked up and said "is there something we can do for you Peter?"

Peter looked at Vinchenzo saying "Marcella and myself would ask you gentlemen to excuse us as we are still rather tired from our experiences of the last few weeks and ask that we may leave you gentlemen to your brandy and cigars."

Vinchenzo looked up and smiled, "of course Peter we understand, good night and we will see you in the morning."

When Peter and Marcella left the room and the and men were sure they had retired, Vinchenzo and the other men returned to the study for further talks, as they felt there were still things to sort out that need not include Peter and Marcella, for instances there was Von Helga, and his squad of goons to deal with as well as the Russian Mafia to consider it was agreed that these were formidable enemies and should not be underestimated.

Gustava, and Michael suggested "that they should pay Von Helga a visit with a few chosen men, to find out what he knows, as to the kidnap attempt on Peter and Marcella, this seemed to be a very informed operation indeed, he had to have had inside information."

Vinchenzo agreed and said "he believed that there was an inside source!", he would therefore return to Bonn in the morning to allow his return to the Vatican to look as natural as possible, it would seem he was finally returning from his sabbatical with Father Angus, who was working with Vinchenzo and the others on this campaign.

Father Angus was covering for Vinchenzo so as not to arouse suspicion as to his whereabouts.

Vinchenzo then said "Abdul, and John would go to Israel, to seek out a friend they knew in Mosad, the Israeli secret service and try to find out if they were aware of any investigation into the "Kristos File", as they would be the first to know if anything was happening, with this operation."

The Mosad where the best in the business next to the British secret service, they would be invaluable at times like these.

Vinchenzo then went on to say, "Hindrich and Franz, you take Peter and Marcella, with you to Moscow and see what you can pick up on the grapevine there, concerning this matter, and that means any information about at all, especially about any unexplained disappearances, and gentlemen be discreet! we don't want to draw unnecessary attention to ourselves do we!", the men all nodded in agreement.

Ivan, was to co-ordinate operations from here and would be on stand by to move in with assault troops should anyone be captured. Ivan was ex special forces and his team were ex specials, some from the S.A.S, and S.B.S some from the Russian, Specials as well as a number from the Israeli intelligence services.

All of these men were willing to die for the cause, they knew the importance of this and were truly committed, they would stop at nothing to retrieve the map and therefore, retaining the secret of the scrolls.

Vinchenzo, suggest "hat they too should retire now and prepare themselves for what lay ahead and God willing their eventual retrieval of the map!" all agreed. Vinchenzo, pulled on the cord near the fire place, the back of the fire place opened to reveal a passage way, the men left through it, it led to a catacomb in the depth of the garden where the men could leave without being seen, it was used as an escape route for the priest in the time of the reformation when the priest were in danger of losing their lives if found. It was also used to hide members of the royal household during the time of the English civil war, when Cromwell's armies would be searching for anyone who was seen as loyal to the king.

The passage was long and dark, not the place to be found in after midnight one thought to himself, however it was most effective in its use, as no one used it these days unless absolutely necessary.

Vinchenzo closed the entrance to the passage by pulling on the cord again, he turned off the lights in the study and left the room shutting the door behind him, he went up the stairs to his room, where he thought to himself its been a long day, Vinchenzo poured himself a brandy, just as a night cap you understand, to help him sleep, however sleep was never a problem for Vinchenzo, but the thought that he may need this night cap to help him sleep was a nice thought, he thought to himself, as he sat in a large armchair positioned in the corner of the room near to a large fireplace. Taking his brandy in one hand and his cigar in the other he slouched back in a relaxed sort of way, enjoying the peace and tranquillity of the moment, the silence was bliss he could feel himself drifting off into a deep relaxing sleep, just then Jenkins, entered the room, he took the cigar out from between Vinchenzo' fingers, then he took the brandy glass which was almost empty by now from his other hand, he gently covered Vinchenzo with a blanket from off the foot of the bed and left the room.

Vinchenzo woke the next morning, he rose from the chair, Jenkins entered the room, with a hearty smile and an even heartier "good morning, did you have a comfortable night m'lord?" he asked, "Yes" replied Vinchenzo, "Considering I was in the chair all night, better than the floor I suppose?"

Jenkins smiled, "yes m'lord I suppose so", replied Jenkins, "would m'lord like me to run his bath now?"

"Yes please" replied Vinchenzo, "then pack my case, I'm off back to Rome on the three o'clock flight, have Anderson and the car ready to take me to the airport at eleven!"

"Certainly m'lord, will that be all?"

"Yes thank you Jenkins, that will be all for now" Vinchenzo replied, and Jenkins left the room.

After Jenkins, left the room, Vinchenzo went for his bath, later he met the others in the dinning room, where Peter and Marcella had already started to tuck into breakfast. Vinchenzo, greeted everyone with a cheerful good morning, asking everyone if they had, had a restful night he then sat at the head of the table he began by saying grace, "for the food we are about to consume may the Lord bless us A-men."

Peter and Marcella froze at the table as Vinchenzo spoke, Marcella, looked at Peter and said very quietly "'oops' I forgot about grace."

Peter looked at Marcella and smiled, "don't' worry" he said "I'm sure Father Vinchenzo will forgive you."

"Yes" Marcella replied, "I'm sure your right!" The men ate breakfast then retired to the drawing room to finalise what was to happen, Vinchenzo had gone over the plan from the night before with them, instructing each group of their mission. Vinchenzo told Peter and Marcella, "they were to accompany Hinerich and Franz, to Moscow!"

"That's Russia" said Marcella! "I've never been to Russia he replied."

Peter just smiled as did the others, "you'll love it" said Peter.

"Will?" I replied Marcella, "isn't it cold there?"

"Only in winter" replied Ivan.

Marcella looked at Ivan, "that's good" he said "I hate the cold!"

Vinchenzo, concluded the meeting with a prayer of protection and blessing, the men all said their farewells and dispersed, then Peter and Marcella, went to their rooms and packed for the journey ahead, their wardrobes were packed with loads of new clothes which had been bought for them shortly after their arrival at the house, Peter had assumed this had happened when they were resting, their clothes must have been taken and the sizes retrieved, this would explain the sudden appearance of a wardrobe full of clothes which fitted almost perfectly.

The men began to pack, Marcella thought to himself to take some warm clothes just in case it was cold as he thought to himself better to be prepared than be caught out. They arrived downstairs almost simultaneously, they put their case down in the hall way and went into the study to say goodbye to Vinchenzo and the others, they entered the room but no one was to be seen, the house was empty, they search high and low for Jenkins, and the others but no one was there, as they re-entered the hall Peter noticed a tray on the table in the centre of the hall, on it was a letter addressed to them both, he thought funny I didn't notice that when we came down, he opened it, it was rather thick for a normal letter, inside was a note, two airline tickets and money the note said dear Peter and Marcella, in this letter you will find all you need for your journey, I am sorry we were unable to stay and say our farewells but time is of the essence in this case, have a safe journey, signed Vinchenzo.

Peter, looked at Marcella in a puzzled way, Marcella said, "well what did it say?" Peter, just handed him the note, just then there came a knock at the door, in walked a rather short haggard gentleman, who said "taxi for Fraggette", this was Peters surname, Peter said "that's me", the man looked at Peter and said "good!" he then took the men's cases and put them in the car, the men just followed a bit puzzled at what was going on, Peter thought for a moment I wonder where Hindrich, and Franz, were, were we not to go with them? How will we know where to find them? All these questions and more were running through his mind.

the taxi driver got in the car, he looked at Peter and Marcella with a puzzled look, just then the driver asked, "is it to the airport sir?"

Peter replied "that's right", the airport if you please, the men got into the car and as they drove away the driver asked them what they had been doing in that deserted old house.

Peter and Marcella looked at each other, in a bemused way, "deserted, you say!"

"Yes" the driver replied, "no one has lived their since the murder of Lord Southerby, in 1945, they say he was assassinated by professional hit men looking for some sort of map."

Peter, looked at Marcella, and motioned with his head to say nothing, Peter, replied "'o' we were just walking along towards the town, and phoned you from the telephone box down the road, when we saw the house so we thought the house would be the easiest point of reference for you to pick us up from."

The driver smiled, "foreign gentlemen are you? Don't tell me Italian."

"Yes that's right" replied Peter, "how could you tell?"

"'O' you know, I was in Rome at the end of the last war as it happens, I was one of Lord Southerby's men during the second world war, we helped liberate Rome from the Gerri's you know, I was wounded four times, once in the arm and three times in the blasted right leg, hence the limp."

"Yes" Peter replied "I noticed that, so where, were you in Italy?"

"Near the Vatican" he said, "we were to stop the Gerri's moving religious artefacts out of the Vatican at all cost and we did for most part, however on one or two occasion they manage to get through but then you can't win them all can you!"

"No I suppose not" Peter replied, just then they pulled up at the airport.

"Well that will be £15-00 please gentlemen."

Peter paid the driver with a twenty and said keep the change, "thanks very much" the driver said, "and if you care to visit us again here's my card, my wife and I run a bed and breakfast just down the road from were you where, its not much but its homely" he said.

Peter thanked him, taking the card from him and assuring him if they returned they would most certainly contact him. The driver smiled and drove away, the two men picked up their suit cases and went in to the departures building, Peter, looked at their tickets, they were for British Airways flight 286 to Domodedovo Airport Moscow, leaving at gate six, he looked up at the check-in board and said to Marcella, "quickly now, this way we've not much time."

Just then Peter, heard a voice calling for passengers for B.A flight 286 to proceed immediately to their boarding point over the public address system, as this was the final call for passengers departing on British airways flight 286 to Domodedovo, would all passengers please go immediately to gate six and to have their boarding passes at the ready.

The men ran down the long corridor to the gate, they just made it with moments to spare; they boarded the plane and made themselves as comfortable as possible, before reclining back into the wonderfully comfortable seats of the plane. Peter, lay back reflecting on the events of the previous few weeks, he thought, I wonder what happened in that house, it was most certainly lived in when we were there it was not derelict by any means and what happened to Jenkins the butler? These questions kept rolling around his head he looked over to Marcella, who was sound asleep by now. Peter began to think to himself once again, I hope nothing happens to Marcella he's a good sort and doesn't deserve to have anything horrible happen to him, besides he's still very young yet.

Peter thought a lot about what had happened since that beautiful summers morning two weeks ago when Angelo, brought the piece or papyrus in to the office how things had changed since then, more to the point how would things turn out, a sudden shiver came over him, he felt a cold yet clammy feeling come upon him, he turned his head towards the window feeling uneasy as if something was going to happen that would leave a lasting scar on his life, he wasn't sure, how, when, or where, this would happen but he felt it would.

Peter, thought enough of this foreboding nonsense! I must be strong for Marcella's sake, and put this nonsense out of my head, Peter lay back and closed his eyes, remembering the lazy summer day's they had back in the square near the Vatican, when he ,Marcella, and Vinchenzo would sit in the sun outside the café, planning their next assignment, that had landed on Vinchenzo desk that Monday morning, or the priority decipher that would occasionally appear on the desk, and the hive of activity this would bring.

Peter wondered if he would see those days again, or for that fact see the Vatican or Rome again, he was suddenly aware that he was slipping back into the foreboding mode again, he quickly rejected such thoughts and began to think once again about his happier memories.

Peter opened his eyes to find the steward asking him if he would fasten his seatbelt as they would be landing shortly, Peter, shook Marcella very gently so as not to startle him, Marcella opened his eyes, Peter just smiled at him and said "it's time to fasten your seat belt we'll be landing shortly."

Marcella stretch in the seat, he gave a rather loud and haughty yawn, and nodded to Peter, Peter could see the runway of the airfield where they would land for the first time, as the aircraft changed course and headed for its final approach to land on the runway, "it wont be long now Marcella" said Peter, "I can see the airport."

Marcella glanced out of Peter's, window and replied "yes I can see it too!".

The aircraft hit the tarmac with a sudden thud, the engines roared once again, the brakes applied and the aircraft came to a gentle halt everyone seemed to stand all at once, Peter and Marcella just sat there waiting for people to clear the isle eventually the aircraft emptied, Peter and Marcella, were the last to leave the aircraft, they walked along the long concourse to where the immigration and passport section was, Peter, told Marcella to have his passport ready, both men approached the man at the desk, he took their passports and taking a long hard look at the men he asked "business or pleasure?"

Peter replied "pleasure."

The man once again took a long hard look at them both before giving them their passports back and saying welcome to Russia gentlemen, and they smiled and walked on.

Marcella looked at Peter, and said to him, "that seemed to take forever."

Peter replied "it did, didn't it, I thought for a moment they knew why we were here, and that perhaps they were going to detain us."

Marcella looked at Peter with a terrified look, and said "I hope not, I don't think I could cope being locked up again."

The two men headed for the exit, but! where they went from there was anybodies guess! Peter decided, what they needed was a good stiff drink so they would go to the nearest café /bar they could find and sit and wait for something to happen.

Peter was sure that something would eventually happen if they waited long enough, the men exited the building, they found a small café not far from the airport there they waited for contact to be made, they had only been there but a short while, just long enough to order their drinks, when a taxi pulled up with a rather portly gentleman in it, the gentleman got out of the taxi, and proceeded to sit down at the table next to them, he order a drink, the taxi waited outside the café, while the portly gentleman ordered a drink, he then finished his drink, got up and started towards the taxi once more, as he past the two men, he dropped a piece of paper into Peters lap but before Peter could say anything the man was in the taxi and he was off.

Peter looked at the screwed up piece of paper and was about to put it in the waste basket near to the entrance door of the café, when curiosity got the better of him, he unravelled the piece of screwed up paper to reveal his and Marcella's name and what looked like a set of directions, the directions were for the men to go to Red Square and stand by the statue of Lenin, where they would be contacted, they were to act like tourist so as to not attract attention to themselves.

First of all though, they were to go over to the taxi rank outside of the airport and wait, a driver would ask them if they had a light, they were to say to him here take this lighter, if he replied I normally use matches they were to accompany him to the car and he would take them to Red Square, the note finished there.

Peter and Marcella got up and went over to the taxi rank, they seem to wait ages before a car drew up, the driver got out and said excuse me do you have a light, Peter said to him "here take this lighter."

The man replied "thank you I normally use matches", the man then said "are you wanting a taxi?"

Peter replied, "yes please!" the men got into the taxi and drove off.

CHAPTER 3
The Moscow Connection

Peter and Marcella had been waiting in the square for some time when Peter, noticed a long black limousine pull around the corner, two rather large men appeared from its interior they wore long black leather coats, just then two more vehicles pulled up and a number of soldiers alighted the vehicles about twenty in all, they headed for where Peter and Marcella stood, Peter froze to the spot as did Marcella, Peter thought to himself that's it we've been rumbled, he grabbed Marcella's hand and with baited breath waited for something to happen, he looked up once again the two men in black leather coats stood in front them, "passports please!" one of them asked.

Peter and Marcella fumbled about their persons to find their passports after what seemed an age they handed the men their passports, the other man said "you will come with us please" the men were led away and put in the back of the truck and driven away.

Meanwhile over at the other side of the square Franz had just arrived to pick up the two men and take them to meet up with Hindrich, as he arrived in the square he witnessed the arrest of Peter and Marcella, he quickly returned to the car which he had parked at the end of a rather narrow alley at the rear of the café so as not to be seen entering the square, he returned to where Hindrich was waiting, Hindrich looked rather puzzled, asking Franz "were they not there?"

"Yes they were there alright" replied Franz, as he began to explain what had happened, when he arrived at the square, Hindrich though for a moment, thinking to himself this is not good, he then turned pausing for a moment he looked at Franz "quickly" he said "we must get in touch with Vinchenzo!"

"How" Franz replied, "he's somewhere in Italy by now."

Hindrich smiled and said "don't worry about that I'll get in touch with him, you use our underground net work to find out where they have taken them."

"Alright" replied Franz, immediately heading for the car, "can I give you a lift anywhere?" he said.

"No!" replied Hindrich, "I've got to go and see somebody close by" he said, the two men left each with a task to do, Hindrich turned back towards Franz, "when you have accomplished your task meet me at Ivan's."

"Alright" replied Franz, "I should be back around early evening if all goes well", Hindrich nodded and they left.

Peter and Marcella, were bundled from the truck some two hours after being bundled into it, they looked up it was some sort of courtyard the buildings towered towards the skyline it was obvious that there was only one way in or out and that was though the main gates which towered fifteen foot high in front of them, the gates where covered with what seemed like little windows with a platform underneath each, these were guarded by men with what looked like machine guns.

Peter and Marcella were led through the courtyard into a doorway then down what seemed endless stairs which led to a long corridor, as they walk they could hear screams as if someone was being skinned alive it was blood curdling to say the least, Marcella was afraid, as he recalled their last encounter with strange men and the fact they had been kidnapped then as well, he began to shake, Peter grabbed his hand to reassure him that he was not alone, Marcella looked at Peter, and said "we are going to die aren't we!"

Peter said nothing, as he thought I don't have the answer to that one, but I'll do all in my power, to avoid such a situation, they carried on down the long corridor, until they came to a door, the taller of the men knocked a voice said enter it was a rather authoritive voice that went right through you, like that of a sergeant major who had got out of the wrong side of the bed and needed appeasing and the only way to do that was for some poor person to be on the sacrificial serving block of life, Peter then thought perhaps Marcella is right this time we will die there will be no heroic rescue this time from this fortress I fear.

The men entered the room, there were in the room three men you could not see their faces as a very bright light aimed towards the edge of the room they entered from this hid their faces in the shadows however, one could make out a uniform, Russian one presumed as they were in Russia Peter thought!

They were told to sit down, Marcella could hardly stand at this point so sitting down was a welcome relief to him, he fare fell into the seat slumping as he did so, Peter on the other hand pulled the chair back and sat quiet majestically compared to Marcella.

There were now five men in the room, the five men gathered together in the corner and whispered as if school children planning an act of mischief, they seemed to be in a long drawn out discussion as to how to handle this situation, Peter thought he heard a name it sounded like Premier Putin, but what would the president of the Soviet Union, want with two decipher clerks from Italy he thought to himself.

Just then Peter could hear footsteps coming towards the room as they drew closer the door suddenly flung open, a silhouetted figure with a military style stance stood in the doorway, the other men seemed suddenly afraid as the man told them to leave the room, that is all except the two men that brought Peter and Marcella to them, the other three men left immediately, the man entered the room he sat across from Peter and Marcella, but they could not see his face only his arms and hands as the light blinded them from seeing anything else the military uniform he was wearing was that of a high ranking officer, but what sort of high ranking officer it was impossible to tell, he began by asking their names and why were they here in Moscow, Peter spoke, saying "they were on holiday, they worked in the Vatican as decipher clerks."

The man slammed his fist on the table, shouting "silence, you will not leave this place until you tell me what I want to know!"

Peter started to speak, just then the man slapped his face saying "silence, speak only when you are spoken too!"

Peter looked towards Marcella, the man had gone over to Marcella, his hand on his holstered revolver, Peter thought no not Marcella again this will finish him, the man stopped short of Marcella, Marcella looked up at the man seeing him near with his hand on the holster, he winced, his hands gripped the edge of the table, he was shaking with fear the man could see this yet he stopped short of Marcella, Peter wondered why as Marcella was obviously the weak link.

Peter watched the man as he paced between the two of them, it was like he was unsure what to do next, the door opened again and another person entered the room, a conversation between the person who came in and the officer already there took place for several minutes, the officer ordered the two other men to take the prisoners to the holding cells, Peter and Marcella were led away.

Hindrich meanwhile; had contacted Vinchenzo, who had given instructions as to what should happen, regarding Peter and Marcella, Hindrich returned to Ivan's house in a shady little suburb of Moscow, Ivan let the other chaps use it as a safe house while he was away, the mafia used the suburb for their drug dealings, so the police avoided it.

The secret police left the area alone, as they were involved in most of the shady dealing that went on in that part of town, therefore it would not be in their interest to go there, that's why Ivan chose it, he had been a K.G.B operative at one time or another and this was one of their former safe houses, so it was handy to say the least, Hindrich arrived back at Ivan's, Franz was waiting for him, "well" said Hindrich "what did you find out?"

Franz began to say, "it looks like they were picked up in a routine sweep and taken to the castle for questioning."

Hindrich said "any chance of them being released routinely."

"Not much of a chance I'm afraid" said Franz, "no one seems to come out of there once they enter it!"

"Can we storm the place!" asked Hindrich?.

"Well normally I would say no! I'm afraid not its too strongly fortified" replied Franz, but then began to say, "however, there is one chance although it's a slim one."

"Yes I'm listening!" replied Hindrich, impatiently.

"Well" replied Franz "there is this old man who says there is an old secret passage into the castle from the lake."

"Yes! Yes! go on" said Hindrich who was now getting rather more impatient.

Franz continued "it was used during the war by peasants to shelter from the bombs."

"Is this old man reliable?" asked Hindrich, who had calmed down by now.

"I think so said Franz!"

"Good then we'll go in tomorrow night, organise it Franz will you."

Franz agreed, "good" said Hindrich "time to have a good nights sleep first, then we'll deal with the problem in a more sober way tomorrow!"

Peter and Marcella meanwhile, were shoved into a dingy room with little light once again, they huddled up in a corner together wondering what was going to happen to them, Peter hugged Marcella trying to reassure him everything would be alright, but Peter knew it wasn't alright, he knew this time they really could die, Peter tried to remove the thought from his head, but it wouldn't go, he just kept think of home and the beautiful life he led in Rome, he hadn't really consider how good life had been to him up until that moment he had always taken these things for granted, he vowed there and then he would never take anything for granted again and should he and Marcella survive, he would devote his life to enjoying all he had in life.

Peter began to wonder what had happened to Hindrich and Franz, he remembered that Vinchenzo had told them that they would meet Peter and Marcella in Moscow, Peter had assumed the instructions were from them, then he thought what if I was wrong and the instructions weren't from them at all, he thought to himself don't be silly of course they were from Hindrich and Franz, no one else but the group new of the plans, and besides if that interrogating office new why they were here he would never have asked us why we were here, this gave Peter a warm feeling of hope, as he knew the others would get them out if they were still at liberty but then he thought, but what if they are prisoners also after all as they were being brought along the corridor they could hear people screaming, suddenly Peter shook himself saying now that's enough, we are going to survive he said to himself, we are going to get out of here!.

The next day Franz organised the assault force into three sections, Franz had been a Legion officer, a highly thought of tactician in the world of espionage, he was seen by many of his contempories as the greatest the world may have ever seen, that's why he organised the assault groups.

Franz began by saying "each group would consist of five men and one officer, they would go in, under cover of darkness, each group would have a specific target, once this target was reached they would deploy as necessary, the communications room must be taken first, this would neutralise communications as far as possible and eliminate the possibility of the radio being used for reinforcement, if word got out then they had fifteen minutes in which to spring Peter and Marcella, as it would take reinforcements seventeen minutes to reach the castle, this would give them two minutes to leave the castle before the reinforcements arrived."

Hindrich asked "are you sure that's enough time."

"Yes" replied Franz, he continued "once the communications room was secure, team two would move into action, taking out the guards on the parapets, this would have to be done quickly and silently therefore, cyanide dipped quarrels and crossbows would be used this was quick and silent, this style of elimination would be effective at 100 meters once all the guards were taken out team two would proceed to secure the perimeter, team three would then go into action, their mission to locate Peter and Marcella and bring them to the surface, taking out any opposition in the process, all three teams would then gather at the entrance to the tunnel and leave the same way they arrived."

Si commented "by the time any body realised what had happened they would all be on a plane to Buenos Aries."

Just then Hindrich appeared with an old map of the castle, "will this help?" he said. Franz smiled, "well actually, we already know the layout as Nicholas, here has been our spy within the Castle for some years now we thought it prudent that we should have someone inside the castle since the early nineties just in case you know we were forced into a predicament like this!"

Hindrich looked at Franz and said "why does that not surprise me!"

Franz looked at him and replied "nice thought though" and smiled, "right where was I, 'O' yes" he said and turned towards two men standing near to him, "make sure you are in the air as backup just in case we need fire cover."

The men nodded, Franz turned again to a smartly dress man saying to him "Sebastian have the plane fuelled and ready for the off at zero three five precisely, if we are not there take off immediately!"

The Hindrich piped up "is everyone clear on their duties?"

With a loud roar the reply came back "yes sir!"

These men were battle hardened veteran with discipline written all over them, they had to be to qualify for service these were as good as they come, when it came to covert operations.

Franz, suggested, "they should regroup back at the flat at twenty one hundred hours for final brief and embarkation."

They all agreed and dispersed. Hindrich asked Franz "if there was anything else he needed?"

Franz said "no, not for the execution of the operation, but it was imperative that the others were on the aircraft by zero two five and no later."

Hindrich reassured Franz that all would be done according to the time table, they would be aboard the aircraft and ready for take off as soon as they arrived with Peter and Marcella, Vinchenzo would be waiting for them, on our arrival in Rio.

"Good!" said Franz, "I'll see you tonight then", Franz left the room, closing the door behind him he proceeded to the airfield to make sure of the final preparations and tie up any last minute loose ends that may occur, Franz was meticulous in his preparations and this operation would be no exception.

Back at the fortress, Peter and Marcella were being taken for further interrogation, they were led once again down the long corridor, as they approached the door of one of the many rooms that began to appear before them they stopped, Peter, was led towards the door, it opened and inside the room was a table with a small man sitting at it he was smoking a cigarette with what looked like a small mother of pear handled cigarette holder on the end, Peter, was shoved down in the chair, and the door slammed shut! Peter thought to himself why is Marcella not here, Marcella, was led to another room a few feet away he entered to see a woman sitting at the table in the middle of the room she smiled and said "sit down please."

Marcella looked in amazement, she was beautiful he thought to himself, she began by asking him again why was he here in Moscow?

Marcella remembered what Peter had told them the day before so he repeated the story, "we are here on holiday."

The woman rose from the table, and looked him straight in the eye and smiled, "look you don't want me to have to get rough with you! do you?.." Marcella, froze for a moment, there was something cold in her voice that he didn't feel comfortable with he shook his head, "good" she said, "so we'll start again shall we?" Marcella nodded.

Marcella thought to himself, I'm not cut out for all this rough stuff , the woman began again "what are you really here to do?"

Marcella repeated his first answer, the woman's face turned from a friendly smile to a look of horror, she slowly rose from the seat and beckoned the two men with her to come forward and hold him, she went to the far side of the room where a kettle was boiling; she took the cloth that lay beside the coffee jar and lifted the hot kettle, she started towards Marcella, as she reached him she said "you should have accepted my generosity!" then beckoning the men to hold Marcella down, they grabbed Marcella, holding him in a tight grip holding his arms out, she began very slowly to tip the kettle towards Marcella's arms and hands, Peter, could hear Marcella's screams, they were blood curdling at best, Peter shot up out of the chair and cried out in a loud voice Marcella's name.

Peter then slumped back into the chair, his head in his hands, he was exhausted from the events of the last few days the man said to him, in a low comforting voice "now Peter if you tell me what you are really doing here, I can stop all this suffering for your friend Marcella, and we have the facilities, to make him well again, but if you do not help, well there's nothing I can do."

Peter, just sat there listening to the screams that were piercing the air around him what are they doing to poor Marcella he thought.

Just then the door opened to the room that Peter was in, the women entered she had come from Marcella's room, she whispered something the man rose from his chair beckoning the men with him to take Peter back to the holding cell, as they led Peter out, he watched them enter the room next door where he had heard Marcella's cries coming from, he wondered what was wrong, what had happened to make the man react so quickly to the woman's intervention? did Marcella, break under the pressure of torture? Or was he dead? Peter had this foreboding a feeling of dread, the men led Peter back to the room from whence they had taken him and Marcella from, as they opened the door they pushed him into the cell, locking the door behind them.

It was awhile later Peter, heard footsteps heading in the direction of the room he was in they stopped outside of the door, Peter thought maybe they are bringing Marcella back, just then the handle began to turn, and then stopped, it released to its original position and the footsteps moved away quickly back down the corridor fading out with every step.

Peter hung his head in his hands thwart with worry, what had they done to Marcella? he thought, how could they be so cruel to a poor helpless; even innocent man like Marcella he would never hurt anyone he was the type of person who would never hurt a living creature not even a fly, Peter, had often witnessed Marcella in the office pick up a spider rather than kill it, he would put it on the window ledge outside the office, or if it were a fly, he would try to catch it or guide it towards the nearest open window he was a harmless soul to all, how could they hurt him?.

Back at Ivan's place Hindrich, and the five other members of the group were preparing to leave, the men had packed and were about to get into the cars to go to the airstrip.

Hindrich, meanwhile had removed all evidence of the men ever being there, when Vladimir, who was the keeper of the safe house and a personal friend of Ivan turned up, Hindrich said to him "to wait for the others to arrive then clean and lock up after they leave."

Vladimir nodded and the men left for the airstrip, Franz returned to the house were Vladimir informed him of Hindrich situation, Franz thanked Vladimir for his help, just then the other members of the group arrived they proceed to the sitting room, where the planned layout of the castle lay, the men finalised their plan and departed to the airfield for equipment issue.

Franz asked Vladimir, "if he would kindly dispose of the plan and tidy up before leaving."

Vladimir smiled and said "certainly sir it will be a pleasure."

Vladimir was a trusted compatriot of the "Guardians", he would make sure no one would ever know any one had ever been there, Franz left in a separate car to the others and the men arrived at the airfield, which was situated approximately twenty minutes from the lake and the entrance to the castle.

The aircraft was on the runway fuelled and ready to go by the time the men arrived at twenty two hundred hours (10pm), the men proceeded to the hanger where the quarter master for this particular operation was waiting with the necessary equipment, each man was issued with their choice of weaponry then they joined together once more to finalise operation crossbow before they left for the castle.

They arrived at a secluded point on the lake no one ever came here as it was through a gate with a sign saying firing range, danger unexploded munitions, this kept un-welcomed visitors out, the men took up their positions and entered the passageway up to the castle it was dark and damp it was obvious this had not been used in many years, that was good thought Franz as this would confirm the element of surprise was on their side as none of the people in the castle would be aware of this entrance.

Franz and the rest of the men reached the top of the stairs, Franz lifted his hand in a motion for the men to stop, they froze clinging to the wall, several of the men knelt with weapons covering all the angles of possible attack, Franz motioned with his hand again, two men got up and joined Franz at the hidden doorway of the passage, they very slowly pushed on the door, as it moved it started to groan, quickly the men stopped pushing, one of the men took a small can from his jacket, he opened it and began to pour the contents on the hinged areas of the door, once again they began to push, this time the door was silent on opening, two more men moved forward and entered the hallway they stayed in a crouched position, a voice came back, "clear" the others moved forward, across the hall and to the left was the communications room, the first squad of men moved towards it as they surrounded the entrance of the room they could see two men sitting at the desk they were both with their backs to the door, however, Si, motioned to the others to wait, the others looked on waiting for the signal to move they only had two more minutes to secure the communications room. Just then Si, noticed a shadow coming from behind an enclosed area of the room that was out of the line of sight, he motioned to one of the men to enter the room from the other door that was just around the corner, the man quickly moved into position, then the signal to move was given they would use silencers to take out the personnel inside, the two men near the entrance to the doors rolled into the room, several small thud like noises were heard and within what seemed a split second the men inside were eliminated, it was very methodical and clean, they never knew what hit them.

Si, motioned to Franz the all clear, Franz motioned the second team into action, they moved into the agreed positions Carl, would be the shooter, Hans would be the loader and the rest would be ready to take out any intruders that may happen along and give Hans and Carl fire support if needed.

Hans loaded the crossbow and handed it to Carl, Carl took aim at the first target, he had to be quick once he had released the first quarrel as the other two guards would see him fall if they were doing their job properly that is, but there was no room for complacency here.

Carl fired, it hit the guard in the neck, he fell instantly to the ground, quickly Hans, handed him the second bow he took aim and fired the second guard was down he then took hold of the third bow. This Hans had loaded while Carl took out the second target, Carl took aim, just then the third guard looked up to see the other two men on the ground Carl fired the man hit the deck rolled over and landed in the courtyard, to the surprise of a fourth man patrolling the yard area, quickly Hans took his revolver leapt from the parapet and let loose two volleys, the fourth man fell in a heap on the ground it was all over in moments Hans, swept the area for other possible intruders then gave the all clear to Carl, who motioned to Fans to go ahead.

Franz and the other team went into action, they followed the planned out lay of the castle to where they thought Marcella and Peter would be, they moved swiftly and silently, Franz looked at his watch they were on schedule but time in this case was of the essence, they moved along the corridor removing any opposition with such precision it was frightening.

Down the hall Franz noticed a room with its door open and voices coming from it, he motioned the men to stop! the men crouched with weapons ready they swept all possible areas were intruders could enter, Franz, once again motioned two men to move forward, they moved in to position one on each side of the door Franz moved up to look, there were several targets inside, Franz put his finger to his throat and motioned to kill all inside the men nodded to each other as if to say now, both men rolled into the room once again several dull thuds were heard, and the groans of several people the men had completed their mission.

In the room lay the woman and man who had interrogated the prisoner and three rather large stocky men all had been shot once in the head, the woman had a look of surprise on her face yet the others were totally unaware of what was happening their facial expressions told that story, Franz and the others moved down the corridor towards the holding cells, just then two guards appeared coming from another room, the men had their backs to Franz and the others, Franz, once again motioned to the two men to go forward however, this time he put his hand on his knife, the two men very slowly approach the guards, as they did one of the men turned: the surprise look on his face told the whole story the men quickly pulled their knives and before the guard could say anything they had pulled the knives across the front of the men throats, they slump't motionlessly on to the floor, Franz, motioned to the two men with him to check the room, they approached the door way just then the door began to open again, Franz put his hand sharply down to motion to the men to get down, the men got down and were ready to pounce when the door shut again, once again they could hear voices coming from inside the room Franz motioned to two of the men to stay at the door, he motioned the other two to follow him, the men took up their positions Franz, continued with two of the men down the corridor time was running out, they hurried to were a single guard was at the entrance to a room, Franz stopped and said to the men very quietly "this must be it, get ready!"

One of the men got on his belly, while the other crouched ready to pounce on the word of command.

Franz checked his watch once more, then motioned the men into action the man crouching moved forward he then threw his knife, it hit the guard in the side of the neck severing the garrotted artery he fell to the ground holding his throat, he lay their dying so the other man shot him in the head this was more humane than him taking several minutes to die, Franz opened the door Peter was curled up in the corner of the room, Franz, knelt beside Peter to see if he was alive or dead, Peter opened his eyes he looked up, seeing Franz, he threw his arms around his neck "I knew you would come."

Franz smiled at him "well come on" he said "we have to be quick, where is Marcella?" he asked Peter.

Peter replied "I am not sure, they put us in separate rooms then I heard Marcella voice screaming out with pain, after that they returned me here to my cell I thought they would bring him back to the cell as well."

Franz looked anxious, for a moment then told the other two men to help Peter to get up, but Peter said "that won't be necessary I'm ok."

"Good" said Franz "lets go."

The men made their way back along the corridor, to where the other men lay in wait, Franz told the two men at the door "to enter and take out any hostile in there, but to protect friendlies if any", they nodded, Franz was hoping Marcella was still alive and in that room! the men entered and eliminated all hostiles then one of the men came out and whispered something to Franz, Franz, motioned to Peter to come to him, Peter moved towards Franz a sudden chill came over him he said "its Marcella isn't it?" Franz looked at him "its not pretty" he said, "they have tortured him I'm afraid, he's beyond help, but he told them nothing!" then he turned and nodded to one of the men, the man knew what he had to do without being told, he turned and head once again for the door.

Franz then took Peter to one side and said "its best put him out of his misery I'm afraid."

Peter asked if he could see him, "best not said Franz, just make matters worse."

Peter started to weep and nodded, Franz nodded to the man at the door a dull thud was once again heard the man returned and shut the door to the room behind him. Franz put his arm around Peter and with a smile said "come on time to leave now Marcella, is in no more pain now."

Franz and the others met at the entrance to the passage, "quickly" he said "we are thirty seconds behind schedule", the men quickly evacuated the building and headed for the trucks and the airfield, and they arrived with moments to spare and boarded the aircraft immediately.

Hindrich, asked Franz "how it had gone?"

Franz told him "of Marcella and how he had been tortured, other than that it had gone according to plan."

Hindrich went over to Peter to try to console him, Peter thanked Hindrich for his kind words but said "he really felt he needed time to himself right now."

Hindrich said "he understood but if there was anything he could do just ask and it was there."

Meanwhile Franz, had gone to the cockpit, the pilot said "orders sir?", Franz replied "lets get out of here before the alarm is given, we have left a bloody calling card tonight."

The pilot smiled, "ok, lets get air bourn, take your seat sir we are about to take off, where are we headed for sir?"

Franz said "use flight plan omicron."

"very well sir!" replied the pilot, the aircraft began to move down the runway it wasn't long before the were on their way the two helicopters were already airborne and heading for the refuelling point that was predesignated in flight plan omicron. They had been in the air about an hour when the orange light came on, this was a warning that something was wrong, only Franz and Hindrich knew this though, so both men arose from their seats and went towards the cockpit, on entry, the pilot looked up and said "we have hostile company a single Mig, fighter, and he closing fast."

Franz said "alert the choppers on the scramble frequency, but don't let the Mig know! just act normal, just in case its nothing."

"Very well sir."

Franz said "the Mig; was approaching from the East, the choppers from the West, so with any luck the Mig would in all probability not notice the choppers as he would be concentrating on them if he was after them in particular."

The Mig flew alongside of them and hailed them to land, the pilot put his thumb in the air as if to acknowledge him then from nowhere one of the choppers appeared, the pilot of the Mig looked astonished he peeled off to starboard and the chopper followed, the Mig seemed to lose control in an instance then in a flash turned into a ball of flame, the chopper returned to its position alongside the aircraft and motioned a thumbs up sign.

The aircraft and choppers crossed over into Turkish airspace then proceeded to the refuelling point situated just inside of the Saudi Borders at a location only know to a few people, it was an underground fuel dump, left by the Gerri's in World War Two, it had been out of use since 1944 but was so deep underground that the allied bombers were unable to locate it, it had a secret entrance that opened up to reveal an old rocket launch pad, the choppers could easily use this for refuelling however, the plane would land some four kilometres away on an old airstrip, where fuel would be waiting for them.

The aircraft landing lights came on the fasten safety belt light lit up, the aircraft began to descend, Peter could see the landing lights of the strip up ahead, he braced himself for the landing but before he knew it the aircraft was down safely and then came to a halt.

The place was a hive of activity, men running to and fro it wasn't long before the aircraft was refuelled and on its way again, it was about an hour later that Franz called Hindrich over, Peter, could just about hear what was being said, Franz had informed Hindrich that Vinchenzo had been on the radio to tell them the planned landing strip had been compromised and that they should change heading, "where to?" asked Hindrich, in a voice that showed no emotion.

Franz replied "we are to rendezvous at point zero."

Hindrich eyes brow lifted, "point zero you say?"

"Yes" replied Franz, "I thought the same thing!"

Hindrich, smiled "at last were going home", both men although surprised seemed pleased.

Peter could not help thinking about poor Marcella, the cries from that room just got louder and longer, they tore at Peter's heart and soul, he wished all this had never happened, then he thought to himself, no I must not think that, Marcella knew the dangers as well as he did, and they both had the option to pull out, but they agreed to carry on until the bitter end, just then the aircraft turned to port, they were heading north, Peter began to think once again about Marcella, and how he loved to go to places he had never been before, he would have loved this Peter thought to himself.

Hindrich and Franz had gone in the direction of the cockpit, they entered the cabin, the pilot looked at them, and said "orders sir?"

Franz looked at him and said, "Head for the rendezvous at point zero."

"Yes sir!", the pilot had already made the course change in anticipation of that very order being given.

Hindrich, went back and told the men of the change in flight plan, a loud cheer came from the men, as if they had been given a huge bonus for their efforts, Peter looked at them, think how good it would be to feel such joy, but the thought of Marcella suffering at the hands of those cruel people, just made him angry, he lay back in his seat feeling numb from his experience, he just wanted to go to sleep and wake up to find all this had been a nightmare, but deep in his heart he knew this would not be the case.

Hindrich returned to the cockpit, Franz turned to him and said, "well we might as well settle down for the long trip home, we will try and get some sleep, set the auto pilot and rest as much as you can" said Franz to the pilot and co-pilot.

"Very good sir they" replied, the pilot looked up and said "refuel at the usual spot sir?"

"Yes" replied Franz, "its all been arranged."

Franz and Hindrich, returned to their seats, everyone was told to get some shut eye, the lights went dim and everyone settled down except for two men who stood watch over the others and the cockpit, just in case they needed to wake up the others in a hurry.

Some time later the two men still awake woke Franz and Hindrich, they headed for the cockpit once more, Peter was fast asleep, the men thought this was best considering what he was going through, the pilot turned towards them, and said "we are approaching refuelling point bravo sir!"

"Good!" said Hindrich, he then took out a piece of paper from his pocket and punched in several numbers and letters in to the console computer, then said "send these coordinates."

The pilot pressed the send button, suddenly in the distance a set of lights appeared, the pilot started his decent the men retuned to their seats and the plane landed, it was a bit of a bumpy landing which shook Peter and woke him and the others up.

Franz stood up and said "right you can get out here if you wish and stretch your legs before we carry on to our final destination point."

Everyone arose from their seating positions and alighted the aircraft, Peter included who was feeling rather cramped from his some what long flight.

Peter left the aircraft via the rear exit with Franz and Hindrich; Franz asked Peter "how he felt now?"

Peter said "I'm better but I cant help thinking about Marcella."

"Yes" Hindrich said, "most unfortunate series of events I'm afraid" "what do you mean?" asked Peter.

Franz began to explain to "Peter about the woman who had interrogated Marcella, she had been a notorious torturer, in the K.G.B and specialised in removing the skin from people to make them talk"

Peter said "stop! I get the picture, but she's dead now!"

Franz said "yes she is now, but there are more like her unfortunately."

The men had reached a hanger on the tarmac, they entered it to find Vinchenzo waiting for them, Peter ran to Vinchenzo, and hugged him, Vinchenzo told Peter how sad he was at the news of Marcella, Peter smiled and said "he was brave to the end", Vinchenzo agreed and the men sat around a large table and drank a welcomed cup of coffee.

It wasn't long before the others joined them, and Vinchenzo, began to explain the next part of the plan, "he pointed out that the players in this particular game, were stepping up the pressure to get their hands on the map, therefore they too must step up their game plan, if they were to stay one step ahead of the operation, that's why they must first return to point zero, so as to see where the others were in the plan of events."

Vinchenzo then suggested "that the men should then re-equip accordingly", the men agreed and returned to their respective aircraft ready for deployment, Vinchenzo said to Peter "you will come with me this time."

Peter, just nodded and the men left together, they went out of a side door to a waiting car, from their towards what looked like a factory about five miles from the airfield, Peter noticed as they entered the yard, that their was a submarine moored up about four hundred metres away, they had entered an old ship yard, the car headed for the vessel, it pulled up alongside the submarine, they all got out and boarded the vessel, they were taken below decks immediately, Peter could feel the engines increasing in speed, the vessel was moving.

Vinchenzo saw the look of anticipation on Peters face, he turned and assured Peter all was alright, he was safe now, Peter smiled and felt reassured at Vinchenzo' kind words.

CHAPTER 4
Point Zero the Return Home

Peter and the others had been on the submarine for what seemed an eternity Peter was laying in his cabin, when he was aware of an increase in movement in the outer corridor, men seemed to be moving with purpose, as opposed to the usual human traffic that would pass by at a saunter, 'no' this time, this was different, he got off his bunk and slid open the door, one of the men was about to pass by, "what's going on?" Peter said.

"We are getting ready to dock" at last Peter thought after a week on this old tub I'm ready for a good walk, a man approached Peter, "you're wanted in the wardroom sir, this way if you don't mind."

Peter grabbed his coat and followed the man along the narrow corridor, moving in and out as people passed each other, they came to a door that said wardroom, the crewman said "in there sir."

Peter entered the room, to find Vinchenzo and Franz waiting for him with the others, "good you're here!" said Vinchenzo, "we are about to disembark, I'm afraid you'll need to trust us on this, we have to give you this injection."

Peter asked "what is it?"

Vinchenzo replied "nothing dangerous I assure you, but it is necessary", he said.

Peter nodded his approval and rolled up his sleeve, Vinchenzo and Franz looked at Peter and shook their heads at his offer of a good vain in the arm, Peter suddenly looked at Vinchenzo and replied "you don't mean?" and stopped there! Franz nodded and said "I'm afraid so."

Peter looked at them in a betrayed fashion, but before he could do or say anything, he felt a sharp jab to his buttock and down he went in a heap on the floor, "good!" said Vinchenzo, "put him in the sarcophagus."

The men picked him up gently and placed him inside the cask, then the lid shut. Vinchenzo told the other men to prepare themselves for transfer, the men left the room and preparation began, for the transfer of all on board.

Vinchenzo went to the conning tower of the submarine, he was joined by Franz, Franz, informed him, "all had been prepared."

Vinchenzo, said "good!"

It was several days later when Vinchenzo was called to the conning tower by the captain, "we are approaching our stated destination sir"

Vinchenzo acknowledged the Captain, thanking him, Vinchenzo, used the periscope to manoeuvre the vessel into position, he waited, for a light to appear on the horizon of the sea bed he kept moving forward slowly and waited, just then, the light appeared, "two degrees port" he said.

The submarine turned towards the light, "midships" came the command.

The submarine slowly stopped turning, "half ahead" said Vinchenzo.

The vessel continued to move slowly forward, "five degrees starboard", immediately followed by "midships", the submarine entered what sounded like a large chamber. "Blow all ballast tanks, prepare to surface" said Vinchenzo, the vessel began to head upwards, then the sound of rushing water was heard all around as the vessel as it broke the surface, "crack the hatches" said Vinchenzo, "come Franz, lets go!"

The men emerged into a large chamber, Franz unload the submarine, "get everyone off, Franz!"

Franz nodded, and the remaining crew helped in the work, Vinchenzo said "I'm going to the bridge if you need me."

Meanwhile, Franz started to unload the two sarcophagus, "take these to cryogenics centre four, the rest to cryo centre three as usual."

"Yes sir" replied the crewmen.

Vinchenzo arrived on the bridge of the vessel, "o k captain he said, we're ready", the captain gave the order and the vessel lifted from the seabed, it propelled forward and over the edge of a deep-water trench, it began to submerge into the abyss.

After several days the submerged vessel flashed its lights on and off, shortly after this a signal came back and the vessel approached a cavern it stopped just short of the entrance, after a short pause it started to move towards the direction of the cave entrance, then the cave mouth suddenly began to open the vessel entered the cave, the doors closed behind it and the water seemed to be sucked out, Vinchenzo ordered the men to open the hatches he thanked the captain for his good work and headed for the hatch.

They were in a huge chamber, which looked like the inside of St Paul's Cathedral dome, only much, much bigger, there was a gantry running around the inside and every so often an entrance door, but no obvious view point, the hatches of the submersible opened and the crew prepared the gangway, the vessel began to empty of its cargo and the two sarcophagus', which were put on a carriage that seemed to run towards an entrance door at the far end of the chamber, "quickly now", Vinchenzo said "we must complete our work as soon as possible, take the sarcophagus' to the ready room but only revive Peter for now!, revive the rest of the crew later, and meet me on level N26."

"Yes sir" came back the reply. Franz began the retrieval process, reviving Peter first then each group in turn, the men then went in to the decompression chamber, from there to process level 2, Vinchenzo and the rest of the crew including Franz had acclimatised while waiting to disembark the vessel, everyone else had to be put through decompression and acclimatisation.

Peter woke up to find himself in a rather splendid room, like that of the penthouse suite in the Plaza hotel in Rome, he thought to himself were am I, just then a rather beautiful young lady entered the room, Peter shot up in the bed, being careful to keep himself covered, the young woman said "good morning Peter, my names Angel!" Peter was stuck for words, then he blurted out in a dry sort of way, "h-how do you know my name and where am I, where is Vinchenzo and the others?"

Angel said; "slow down! all of your questions will be answered shortly, but first we must get you up showered and dressed"

Peter, swallowed deeply, "now just a moment!" he said "I'm old enough to shower and dress myself."

Angel just smiled and replied "of course you are!"

Peter got up and dressed, after the wonderful shower he had taken, it wasn't long before Angel returned for him, he was then taken to room N26, were breakfast was being served.

He arrived just in time from the looks of it, they were just about to sit down and tuck in, Peter started to ask Franz "what was going on and where were they?"

When Vinchenzo said "patience Peter! Lets have breakfast first then we'll talk."

Peter was too anxious to eat, he just nibbled at the toast, however, the coffee was a welcome sight, he was on his fourth cup when Vinchenzo rose from the table and said, "Gentlemen please follow me", and everyone got up from their seats and proceeded to follow Vinchenzo out of the room and down the corridor.

The corridor was long with many off shoots and doorways, the complex was huge, but where were they!, Peter thought to himself, they carried on through another, set of doors, then up several flights of stairs, before reaching a door marked conference room "Alpha", level 29, twenty nine levels thought Peter, and there may be even more, where are we, and what is this place? All these questions and more were going on in his mind, he needed answers, and he needed them quickly he thought to himself.

Vinchenzo opened the door to the room with a swipe card, the door gave a hissing sound and then opened, the door was very thick like that of a vault.

The men entered the room, in the room was a very large oval table surrounded by at least twenty rather grand looking chairs, in the middle of the table was what looked like a floating screen the screen just seemed to hang there in mid air, at the far end of the room there was a porthole style window with what seemed to be a rather large aquarium behind it, to the left of the table was a bureau with refreshments on it, to the right of the table was a large cabinet.

The men sat down at the table in their respective seat which had been previously, name carded. Just then another door opened in the far right hand corner of the room, then a person entered, it was Jenkins, he walked up to Vinchenzo, bent his head towards Vinchenzo' ear and whispered something, Vinchenzo rose from his seat saying "you will have to excuse me gentlemen, I'll be back as soon as I can, meanwhile chat amongst yourselves, and feel free to help yourselves to refreshments, Peter would you come with me please."

Peter rose from his chair and followed Jenkins and Vinchenzo out of the room through the door in the corner.

The men entered another large room, this time it was more of a command centre style room, several men sat at various points in the room each with his own work station, it was a hive of activity, something was up Peter could sense the tension in the air, Vinchenzo was in the corner looking into what seemed to be a closed off screen, Peter thought to himself I wonder what's up, just then Vinchenzo turned and walked towards Peter, he looked at Peter and calmly and quietly said, "Peter what we are about to show you, you may find hard to understand, however it is necessary for us, that you know what is going on and that you understand fully the implications of what is happening here."

Peter looked at Vinchenzo not quite understanding what had just been conveyed to him, but nevertheless he nodded in approval, Vinchenzo, began to explain where they were, he said "his place was built by the Germans during the Second World War at a time they were experimenting with nuclear fission in case there was ever a nuclear war. From here they could monitor events on the surface, we are at seven miles down under the "Polar Ice Cap", that is why we had to put you in to a deep sleep to allow you body time to acclimatise to the conditions this far down, it was abandoned some years ago. We are totally undetectable to those on the surface and are in fact invisible by all accounts, even satellite surveillance has difficulty in detecting this station, because of the depth of water and ice this tents to masked us somewhat."

Peter turned to Vinchenzo, and said "so no one knows this is here but us?" Vinchenzo smiled "not quite Peter" he said "there are certain trusted individual that know of this place, however they don't know how to find it by themselves, each one of the seven have a piece of the clue, but no one has more than one piece so no one person knows the true location of the station. That way no one can give its location away not even me, those who live on the station never leave they are, here for the duration."

Peter stopped and looked at Vinchenzo, and said "you mean I'm stuck hear for good?"

Vinchenzo looked at Peter and smiled, "not quite Peter" he said in a reassuring voice, "you don't know the location of were we are only that it is somewhere in the artic circle, no! You will leave here when the time is right in the same fashion as you arrived."

"O' good" said Peter in a relived sigh, once again Vinchenzo smiled and they proceeded to the exit where they entered the corridor once more.

The men came to a lift, they entered it and proceeded upwards, it seemed to take a long while before the lift came to a halt, the doors opened and they entered what seemed to be a large corridor that had been carved from out of a gigantic pearl, it looked like it was going to go on forever, when suddenly it came to an abrupt end, Vinchenzo, and the other man took from their pockets what looked like two keys. Peter thought to himself but there's no door that I can see, why the keys? Then Vinchenzo and the other man knelt down, they place the keys into what looked like the ground and turned together, there was a grinding and groaning noise that seemed to come from the wall in-front of them, suddenly the wall began to move, it seemed to disappear into the other wall as if by some sort of magic it slid slowly across in-front of them revealing what looked like a large city, it spread for as far as the eye could see in every direction, it was ancient in its style yet modern in its conception it was awesome to look at.

It was as if its streets were lined with a golden substance and a river as pure as the driven snow ran through its length, its course was through the middle of the city. The men entered the city they walked along its main street to a building at what would seem to be the centre of the city, here Vinchenzo, told Peter "he must stay close to him and all his questions would be answered, but he must trust Vinchenzo what ever happened."

Peter, swallowed sharply once more and agreed to do whatever Vinchenzo said.

They entered the building; it was like nothing Peter had ever seen the walls seemed to be made from marble, the stairs of the purest gold, the ceilings of the most beautiful pearls you could ever imagine, it was beyond description, Peter thought to himself, it must be an illusion of some kind, he reached out to touch the walls, they felt real enough, he pinched himself as if to wake himself up, yet, he was awake and squinted at the sudden pain he had just inflicted upon himself.

The men continued along the corridor to a room at the end of the long passageway, Vinchenzo opened the door and the men entered in to the room, the room was empty all but for an elderly gentleman sitting in an arm chair with his back to them near the window looking out into the street below, Vinchenzo, bowed to him, Peter was taken back by this, this was not the usual, he thought to himself, he watched as Vinchenzo approached the elderly gentleman, the man did not turn around, Vinchenzo stood before him speaking in a form of long lost ancient dialect, or so it would seem to Peter.

As Vinchenzo spoke so the old man seemed to glow as did Vinchenzo, it seemed, the closer he got to the old man, the brighter he got, until he was so bright, all one could see was the light, Peter rubbed his eyes and said to the other man "I am sure I can make out three silhouettes", the man just smiled, Peter protested to him "I can! I can see three silhouettes", then Peter though but how can that be! there was only two people over there, Vinchenzo and the old man?

The other man just looked on and said "I am sure your right", in a patronising way as if he knew something Peter did not.

Just then the light disappeared and there was Vinchenzo sitting in the chair were the old man had once sat, Peter ran up to the chair, "are you alright Father Vinchenzo?" "Yes quite alright thank you Peter" he replied.

Peter stammered, "b-but where did the old man go? What's going on he said in a puzzled voice?" Vinchenzo assured him he would be told all before he left the station.

They returned to the others, to find them only just starting breakfast, it was like they had only just left the room and immediately returned, yet to Peter they had been gone some hours, Peter was really puzzled by now, but knew Vinchenzo would not let him down and indeed would reveal all to him in time.

Vinchenzo sat at the table and apologised for their absence, the men just carried on with their breakfast as if nothing more than a minor inconvenience had taken place, when they had finished their meal and chatted about different things, Vinchenzo apologised to the men at the table and asked the men if they wouldn't mind leaving the room as he needed time to talk to Peter, they all rose from the table, except for Peter and Vinchenzo, as the men were leaving, Vinchenzo, asked Franz to stay behind with him, Franz sat back down, Vinchenzo, began to tell Peter a little about the history of the order, Vinchenzo explained "the order was an ancient order set up by the priesthood of Melchizedek, these were the kings and priest of Salem, entrusted with the secret treasures of God here on earth, they were the priest of the most high God El (Yahweh), in the time of Abraham of the Jewish, Christian, and Muslim holy books, throughout the centuries."

Vinchenzo then went on to say "our job has been to protect these secrets and stop man from getting his hands on them, that is why man still seek to find them today as he sees them as the ultimate treasure here on earth."

Peter looked at Vinchenzo, he paused for a moment before saying tentatively, "just a minute, just how old are you then?" Vinchenzo looked back at Peter and said in a quiet voice "we are all the same age."

"Yes!" Peter anxiously replied, "But how old are you?"

Vinchenzo asked Peter "does it really matter, the main point is we are who we are and our job is to look after the scroll."

Peter once again asked with urgency in his voice, "how old are you really? this matters to me, how old are you?"

Vinchenzo finally succumb to peters persistent question, "I am 4200 years old approximately that is give or take a century or two", replied Vinchenzo.

"one often loses the sense of time in our position and the odd year is missed here and there."

Peter almost collapsed, stammering he said "f-four th-thousand years old that's not possible."

Vinchenzo looked at Peter and said "in earthly terms your right, but although we are in this world we are not of it, our world is a kingdom world, were love exists in place of greed that's why we can never be tempted by that greed that drives men to kill."

Peter, just sat there glued to his seat, unable to move, then he spoke "does this mean I'm dead and can never return to my former life?"

Vinchenzo and Franz, smiled to one another, "no Franz said, it is only us who are immortal you my friend are still mortal, however, one day you to will join us!"

Just then the door opened at the far end of the room and in walked Marcella, Peter froze, he gripped the arm of the chair with a vice like grip his knuckles turned white with fear, Vinchenzo leant over and put his hand on top of Peters gripped fist, "don't be afraid Peter you are not seeing a ghost as such, it is Marcella, he's real enough ask him, touch him."

Peter shot out of the chair, and fell on Marcella's neck and kissed him, "forgive me" he whispered to Marcella.

Marcella whispered back "there is nothing to forgive Peter."

Peter wept, and said "I thought I had lost you forever."

Marcella, smiled and replied "apparently not!".

Peter was a wreck; he looked at Vinchenzo, and said "how can this be? Marcella, was shot by one of your men because of the pain he was in, he died, I heard it with my own ears."

"Slow down" Vinchenzo, said to Peter and "I will explain everything, it is true Marcella was beyond help in this worlds terms, but we don't deal in this worlds terms, what is impossible to man is more that possible to our superiors, as our superiors have blessed us with powers to heal and raise the dead if necessary."

Peter was astonished at what he heard, he slumped back once again into the chair, exhausted from what he had witnessed, Vinchenzo felt Peter had gone through enough for today and suggested that they should rest now and meet later that day where more answers would come to light.

The men rose from the table and departed each to their own place of rest, time seemed to have no meaning where they were, neither day or night seemed to exist.

Peter and Marcella, went to Peters quarters where Peter asked Marcella "what had happened?"

Marcella, said "he wasn't sure but he would tell Peter all he could." the men spoke for hours, Peter asking Marcella question after question and Marcella trying to appease Peter with the answers he was giving him, but the more Marcella, answered Peter, the more questions Peter seemed to come up with, until both men were exhausted, then Peter flung his arms around Marcella, and the two men just hugged each other, Peter said "its good to have you back", and Marcella agreed it was good to see Peter again.

While the men were chatting, a knock came at the door, the young lady Peter had met earlier entered the room and said "your presence is requested in the conference room please follow me."

The men followed the young lady to where they had met earlier, they entered the room, inside all the other men were sitting waiting for them, "sit down" said Vinchenzo, ""now we are all here we can begin!, Gentlemen, it is time for us to move, and move quickly, we must return to the surface immediately, as things are developing quite nicely I think."

Peter whispered to Marcella, "What is all that about I wonder?" Marcella shrugged his shoulders.

Vinchenzo went on to say, "we leave in an hour, please prepare to get under way immediately, the men rose from the table and left the room, leaving Peter, Marcella, Franz and Vinchenzo.

Peter asked "where are we going and why?"

Vinchenzo replied "you will see soon enough."

Peter whispered to Marcella, "what! More surprises, I'm not sure I can take much more."

Marcella whispered back "its exciting isn't it."

Peter looked at Marcella "you are joking aren't you he whispered?"

Marcella turned towards Peter and smiling said "No"!

Peter put his head in his hands and thought 'o' no, here we go again, Peter and Marcella went to prepare themselves to leave the station.

The met back in the corridor out side of Peters room, while there, they were met by Vinchenzo and Franz, Vinchenzo asked Fran to escort Peter and Marcella to the embarkation area as he had to go and finalise things before leaving, Franz led the men to the submersible that had brought them, they boarded the vessel and were led to a room with capsules in it about twenty in all, Franz, asked Peter and Marcella to get into one each, Peter looked at Franz, he was smiling, this worried Peter as the last time Franz had smiled like that Peter had felt a sharp prick and a warm feeling in his leg, it was just before they left last time.

The men did as they were asked and the doors closed, Peter felt relief that Franz had not stuck him with another needle, just then there was a soft hissing noise, Peter felt himself falling a sleep, then what seemed moments later the capsule door reopened, Peter thought it must have malfunctioned as Franz was still there in that same spot, with that same mischievous smile, Peter rubbed his eyes and alighted the capsule, as did Marcella, Peter turned to Franz, and said "is there a problem, did it not work?" Franz said to Peter.

"O' yes it worked fine", Peter replied "but we've only just got into them and we've had to get out haven't we?"

"Not quite Peter" Franz replied "you've been in there a week!"

"How long?" Peter asked.

"A week" replied Franz.

Peter stood stunned for just a moment, he said "well it didn't feel like a week!"

Franz and Marcella just laughed, Peter thought well I don't know why they are laughing, I've lost a whole week. Franz and Marcella took hold of Peter and led him to where the others were waiting.

Vinchenzo welcomed them back to the land of the living, Vinchenzo began to explain the next part of the plan, "they were to go to Brasilia, the capital of Brazil, where they would leave on the next leg of the journey, however all would become clearer as they began this journey up the Amazon."

Amazon! Peter thought, Amazon!, well at least its warmer than the Artic, that's for certain, just then a man entered the room he headed straight for Vinchenzo, he whispered something to Vinchenzo, Vinchenzo' reaction was to smile, he looked up and said "all is prepared we should now prepare ourselves for the journey ahead of us Franz, are the men in place?"

Franz looked at his watch, and replied "they will be in place in approximately one hours time."

"Good!" said Vinchenzo, "let me know when they are in place."

"Very well sir" said Franz, and left the room.

Vinchenzo then said "Ivan are you ready?"

"Ready as I'll ever be sir." replied Ivan.

"Good then proceed to your station."

"Very good sir" he replied, and he too left the room.

Vinchenzo looked up, and said "now, Gustava and Michael will be there to meet us when we arrive and all the necessary equipment will be in place, now gentlemen I must warn you to be alert at all times as we have just heard that Von-Helgar and his men are in Brasilia as we speak, and are on the trail of the scroll themselves and I need not remind you that he is a very dangerous customer, if he finds Brown first we'll have a devil of a job to retrieve the map, but nonetheless retrieve it we will."

Just then the door opened once more and in walked Jenkins, "the necessary travel arrangements are in place sir, will there be anything else sir?"

"No" replied Vinchenzo, "that will be all Jenkins."

"Very well sir", he replied, and left the room.

Vinchenzo looked up and said "well gentlemen it looks like it is time for us to part company for the moment, therefore it only remains for me to say bon-voyage and good hunting."

The men left the room leaving only Peter and Marcella with Vinchenzo, Vinchenzo looked at the men and reminded them how important it was that they should "stay close to him, however, in the event we do get separate go to this address in the city and await instructions is that understood!"

Peter and Marcella nodded their heads, "right" said Vinchenzo, "meet me on the jetty in half an hour, go now and prepare to leave."

Peter and Marcella headed for their rooms, but as they left the room; they were met by a crew member who was holding their luggage in his hand, the man said "no need to worry sir we've already packed for you at the captains orders, I think you'll find everything you need is in there."

"Thank you" said Marcella "I'm sure your right!"

Peter thought I hope so.

The man said "follow me gentlemen" and he led them up onto he upper deck of the submarine to the gangway and on to the quayside, where everyone else was waiting.

On the quayside were several limousines, the men were told to get in to them and they drove away.

They arrived back at the hanger at the airfield they had originally landed at before boarding the submarine, Peter remembered how they had land and were driven off in to the shipyard were they had started this eye opening journey, he reminisced about what had occurred over the time that had past, he still wasn't sure what was happening other than he had to keep his promise to see this task, whatever it was, through to the end, however he was so pleased to have Marcella back in one piece, that for him was reward enough.

The cars arrived at the air field, the plane was ready for the off, the men got out of the cars and quickly boarded the aircraft, "buckle up", Vinchenzo said, "we've a long flight ahead of us so the sooner we get going the better."

The plain taxied to the runway, suddenly the engines pick up speed and the plane lurched forward, they were off, the ground just seemed to disappear from under them, then they were on their way, Peter thought well, Brazil here we come and then settled back in the snug comfortable seat of the Jet, allowing his thoughts to drift into whatever direction they would take him, he had a long journey ahead of him, and plenty of time to do it in, there was no rush whatsoever: after all he was only rushing to his own funeral he thought, and that could wait as long as possible as he wasn't quite ready to die yet, at least, not with out a fight anyway.

Vinchenzo came over to Peter and Marcella, he gave them each an envelope and said "should you get separated use what is inside these envelopes to get you to a place of retrieval where we can extract you safely ok."

"Ok" Peter and Marcella replied.

Vinchenzo emphasised to them the importance of not opening the envelopes unless absolutely necessary, then he asked them if they wanted anything for the flight, magazine, drink, or maybe a cup of coffee, Marcella said no thank you, I'm alright for the moment.

"Well if you do decide you need anything Marcella just ask, and someone will get it for you", replied Vinchenzo.

Peter on the other hand said yes please as his eye's lit up at the thought of his favourite beverage. Vinchenzo smiled at Peter and said "yes I had a feeling you might say that so I radioed ahead and requested a pot of coffee to be made ready." and headed for the galley where the coffee was brewing, he returned with a mug of coffee for Peter and said "there is more in the pot if you feel you need it."

Peter thanked Vinchenzo, Vinchenzo replied, "that's alright Peter my pleasure I assure you", then head once more for the cockpit of the plane.

Peter still had so many questions in his head and especially about what happened with Marcella, like how on earth did they revive him? Did they really shoot him to put him out of pain? And why are there no scars on his body?, Peter had earlier that day seen Marcella in the shower room his body looked perfect, even the old scar he had as a child had disappeared, it was from falling from a tree as a boy, he had torn his skin on a branch as he fell, he had had to have extensive surgery on it over the years.

Peter had often accompanied Marcella to the hospital, the scaring was quite extensive, yet now it was gone, Peter supped at his coffee, then he thought to himself, well for the moment sleep is more important at the moment and Marcella's eye's are already closed, so time enough for questions latter, but for now sleep I think.

It didn't seem long before Vinchenzo was shaking Peter gently, Peter opened his eye's to hear Vinchenzo reassuring voice saying "come along sleeping beauty! Its time to fasten your seat belt we are landing shortly."

Peter shook himself and fastened his seat belt, the plane was already in the flight path and descending towards the airfield, it was an old U.S Air force landing strip miles from anywhere it would seem, and on the ground Peter could see, a hive of activity, it looked like they were preparing for something big, suddenly, the plane touched down onto the tarmac with a sudden thud and the screeching of brakes, the jet came to a halt directly in front of the hanger where all the activity was going on, Vinchenzo stood up and opened the exit, saying "gentlemen we have arrived please make your way to your allocated stations."

The men got up and exited the jet, Vinchenzo looked at Peter and Marcella and said "follow me please gentlemen."

Peter and Marcella got up and followed Vinchenzo out of the jet and across the tarmac, which was by now filling up with crates of all sizes; it looked like someone was preparing for battle.

CHAPTER 5
The Nest Is Bare

I t wasn't long before the men were joined by Gustava and Michael, who had been finding out what Von-Helgar was up to while they had been at point zero, the men approached Vinchenzo, and began to inform him of their intelligence gathering, they began by telling Vinchenzo that "Von-Helgar had brought in his best assassins on this one, the elite of his henchmen, they were known for their brutality and savagery." "Not to worry" Vinchenzo said "we'll deal with them when the time comes, and the time will come I assure you", he said, "what else did you find out?"

"Well he had hired a number of boats to take him up river but no guides" said Gustava.

"Does that mean he brought his own with him then?" asked Vinchenzo.

"Yes" replied Gustava, "it most certainly looks that way."

Just then a man entered the room wearing a uniform a very official looking man, his uniform had much gold braid on it, Vinchenzo looked up at the man and said, "well Angus how are you, you old coot?"

The man replied in the most broadest Scottish accent, "Och' well you know, 'neigh' bad, how's yourself, fit like I hope?"

Peter just stood there glued like a fly to fly paper, this is the famous Angus, but what is he doing out here?, and even more important what was he doing wearing a military uniform?, wasn't he supposed to be a priest?, wasn't this the famous Father Angus?, that Vinchenzo had told us about so many times in the past? Peter, was at a loss for words, he turned to Marcella with a look of bewilderment, Marcella could see he was rather perplexed over this situation, so he said "to Peter don't worry I am sure Vinchenzo will fill us in on all the details later on", and smiled, this did not seem to help Peter as he still had that look of bewilderment on his face.

Vinchenzo began, "right gentlemen lets get down to business, now you were saying Gustava, Von Helgar has hire a number of boats in the area and on top of that he has brought with him specialist help of his own."

"Yes that's about it sir."

"Right" said Vinchenzo "anything else we need to know at this point?"

Michael, spoke in a gentle soft spoken voice, not the type of voice one would associate with that of a trained assassin, Michael started by saying, "well sir there is one thing, it may be something or nothing, but both myself and Gustava think it is worth mentioning."

"Yes" replied Vinchenzo "go ahead tell us then, nothing no matter how small or insignificant it may seem must be over looked."

Michael smiled and continued, "well gentlemen we came across a native from a little known tribe two days ago, we had difficulty understanding him at first, but eventually realised he was speaking an ancient Canaanite language unspoken for thousands of years, he came from deep in the Amazon jungle, where no white man has set foot for thousands of years until about a year ago. When two men, were found near the village, they were almost dead according to the fellow, however, one man died but the other recovered! that mans name was Brown."

Vinchenzo looked up, "Brown you say?"

"Well as far as we could ascertain yes sir."

"Are you sure Michael", Ivan said.

"Well as sure as we could be, but remember this is an ancient language, and it is all down to interpretation."

"That's interesting Michael", Vinchenzo said, "could this ancient Canaanite language be of Hittite origin?"

"Well it could be, but I can not be absolutely certain, he did wear the mark of Mattock one of the Hittite gods of that time, and that symbol was believed to be the symbol of the high priesthood, not the type of thing one would expect to find these days outside of the Ancient Near East."

"Why is that?" Peter asked.

"Well, Peter" replied Vinchenzo, "Ed-Baal a king around that period, had sent an expedition force to seek out new lands to the North around the second Millennium B.C eventually never to be heard of again. They disappeared from the face of the earth so legend has it, and ancient legend has it as they came to a vast sea of ice, they were rumoured to have crossed it and were never heard of again, now supposing that this was point zero as we know it now, 66* north, if this is so, then they would have eventually arrived at Canada, then America, ending up in the Amazonian jungles of South America!

After all in those days the landmasses of the world were believed; to have been joined together, were they not?"

Vinchenzo paused for a moment in thought, then Vinchenzo, said, "ok thank you Michael, you and Gustava have done well."

"Thank you sir" both men replied.

Vinchenzo went on to say "Now let us move on gentlemen and plan our campaign, Michael and Gustavo, take one section of the men and head up river."

"Franz take the other men and cut across land and cut off Von Helgar, but remember he is a formidable enemy so don't take un-necessary chances."

"Very good sir" replied the men.

Vinchenzo carried on "meanwhile Peter, Marcella, Angus, and myself will head for base camp and prepare to move out in twelve hours with the rest of the men on horse back."

Horse back! Peter thought but I can't even ride, 'O' no, he thought! here we go again, Marcella knew Peter had problems with any animal, so he turned to Peter, and said "don't worry you're in good hands I'll look after you."

Peter felt a flourish of relief come over him as Marcella reassured him, Peter knew Marcella was an accomplished rider and therefore knew what he was doing, although this did not take away all of Peters fears it most certainly helped to give him some comfort.

Vinchenzo asked "are there were any questions about what had been said so far!"

The room was silent, Vinchenzo said "I'll take it from the silence there aren't any questions, therefore, gentlemen you may leave for your necessary assignments and may God be with you all, therefore, all that is left for me to say is dismissed and good hunting."

Peter, Marcella, Angus and Vinchenzo left the room and proceeded to a large white limousine which was parked near the front doors of the hanger. As they walked towards the limousine, Peter asked Vinchenzo about Angus, Peter asked Vinchenzo "was this the same Father Angus from Bonn?"

Vinchenzo suddenly looked at Peter with a rather embarrassed look "oh, goodness me! no its his son, Father Angus is much older than this Angus, no, this is Angus' son, Angus junior."

Peter once again looked at Vinchenzo in a bewildered way "his son?" he said.

"Yes that's right" replied Vinchenzo, "big fellow isn't he, he's just like his father, the uniform is that of head of intelligence in Brasilia, so we should not arouse any suspicion while we are in town."

Peter was even more puzzled now, a Scotsman and a big one at that! Head of intelligence in Brasilia, why? Oh well he thought I am sure there is a perfectly logical explanation for all this; however, it seems to allude me at the moment.

The limousine headed off in the direction of the capital, Vinchenzo had had a mirror fitted that allowed him to look to the rear of the vehicle, Peter noticed he kept glancing into the mirror from time to time then suddenly Vinchenzo, lent forward and spoke very softly to the driver, who immediately pulled over to the side of the road Vinchenzo looked at Angus junior, "why?" he said:

Angus gave out a sigh his face looked startled as if he was suddenly winded and out of breath he slumped forward in the seat, quickly Vinchenzo said "out of the vehicle." The men got out of the car, and headed for the thick brush at the side of the road, Peter could see Ivan and several men laying in the bushes, "quickly now!" said Vinchenzo "this way."

Peter and Marcella hurried in to the brush, there was a screech of brakes then a volley of gun fire, before Ivan returned to say all was safe, Peter looked at Marcella in that bewildered way as if to say "what's happened now?"

Vinchenzo looked at the bewildered look on Peter face and said, "it was a necessary action", and began to explain why such drastic action was necessary, "it appeared that Angus junior had gotten greedy, and was on Von Helgar' payroll those shots were taken care of Von Helgar' assassins, Angus had informed them of our imminent arrival and agenda, but as in all these type of double agent agendas, there is often a leek and we found out just in time about his planned ambush!"

Vinchenzo turned to Ivan and said "are all four in the car and the assailants vehicle dealt with?"

"Yes sir" said Ivan.

Vinchenzo said "good! now go and set the vehicle alight with the bodies in and make sure there is no forensic evidence left, then meet us at base camp, I need not remind you I'm sure Ivan that time is of the essence."

"Very good sir" said Ivan and left to deal with the orders he had received.

Peter turned to Vinchenzo and said "but what about Angus junior, shouldn't you inform his father?"

Vinchenzo looked at Peter and Marcella and said "don't worry I will all in good time, but for now it is enough that we leave this place and get to base camp in one piece."

Just then Ivan returned with some men, "everything ready?" asked Vinchenzo.

"Yes replied Ivan."

"Good then make the call and inform our friend on the media of the ambush and murder of Fergus Angus the chief of the secret police on the road to the capital, and say it was insurgent rebels, fighting for the peoples liberation front, now come lets go!"

The men headed for the river and onto the boats that would take them up stream to the main force were they would spend the night before leaving the next day to the base camp.

The men reached the safety of the main force just in time for supper, Peter flopped to the ground, his day had been an eventful one to say the least, as he lay there he felt something near his neck it felt smooth yet thin and long Peter was just about to put his hand at the back of his neck, when Marcella grabbed it, "don't move Peter" he said very softly, he pulled out his knife, Peter just froze and squinted his eyes, Marcella thrust the knife downwards and pulled up sharply, Peter opened his eyes to see a small snake on the end of Marcella's knife, "'phew' that was close" said Peter. Marcella smiled and said "yes you just don't know how close that was."

Peter asked was it harmless, Marcella smiled and said "actually quite the opposite, one bite from this little fellow and it would be curtains I'm afraid."

Just then Vinchenzo walked over towards them, "right lads a good nights sleep then we leave in the morning for base camp."

"Can't we go now" said Marcella!

"No!" said Vinchenzo "this jungle is far too dangerous to travel through in the dark, far too dangerous", repeated Vinchenzo, "no! We'll leave in the morning that's soon enough" he said, and then he wished them a good night.

A good night! Peter thought to himself I'll never be able to sleep after what just happened, I almost died on my first night in the jungle and he says sleep tight! Yes right! I'm sure I will (not is more like it).

Next morning Peter woke to the smell of Brazilian coffee roasting over a open fire, and a dawn chorus of all sorts of wild life, he quickly got up and headed for the aroma of the coffee, Marcella was already up and coming from the direction of the river whistling in a happy sort of way, "good morning Peter", he shouted.

"Good morning" Peter replied and waved, he sounded a lot less awake and was heading for the coffee,

"I see you like the smell of the coffee?"

"Yes" replied Peter "it smells good!"

""I've already had some it is very good, help yourself."

"Thank you I will" replied Peter.

Peter took a cup and filled it to the top, he sat on a log by the smoky fire, and supped his coffee, holding tight to the cup, thinking to himself well at least I'm alive and the coffee is excellent too, he smiled to himself and thought well this is one the grandchildren will find hard to believe, that is if I live long enough to have grandchildren, he once again savoured the taste and smell of the rich aroma of his coffee.

Vinchenzo, appeared from the direction of the river, "well Peter I hope you slept well? Because we have a long day ahead of us!"

Peter looked up at Vinchenzo, and in a sleepy voice replied "I'll make it."

Vinchenzo smiled and said "I'm sure you will I'm sure you will!"

Just then a voice shouted "ready sir."

Vinchenzo turned to Peter and Marcella who were both around the coffee pot by now, and said "come on, you two time to move."

Peter looked up at Vinchenzo "but I've only had two cups!"

Vinchenzo looked at Peter once more and said "never mind Peter there's plenty of coffee at base camp, but for now we must move, and move quickly, we are about to have visitors I think."

Just then Ivan and some others appeared "they'll be here in an hour he said."

"Good" said Vinchenzo, "have you laid the surprises out for them?"

Ivan replied, "Yes sir, they are all ready for them."

Peter and Marcella thought to themselves I wonder what he means by surprises, they just looked at each other and shrugged their shoulders, right said Vinchenzo, "down to the river with you and get onto one of the boats."

Peter and Marcella got up and headed towards the direction of the river, Peter was still clutching his third cup of coffee which he had refilled while Vinchenzo and Ivan were talking.

Vinchenzo signalled the boats to move off they headed up river, the river at this stage was wide so they kept to the tree line for cover it wasn't long however, before the river narrowed dramatically and they were hidden from all view, Peter was sweating, he felt uncomfortable so he hung his hand over the side of the boat, the water was cool, he felt as if he could just dive in and cool off, suddenly one of the men grabbed Peters arm and said "I wouldn't do that if I were you sir" pointing towards the banks of the river.

Peter could see lizard like creatures sliding into the water either side of the boat, "crocks sir! take a mans arm off at the bone, or drag you in and wedge you between a tree stump on the bottom then eat you later" said the man.

Peter swallowed sharply and in a stammering voice replied "ok I get the message I won't be doing that again."

It wasn't long before the men reached base camp and unloaded the boats, they set up the camp ready for operation, the camp was an old tribal village deserted long ago because of sickness the local tribes were superstitious, and would not re-inhabit a village where death caused the demise of that village they saw it as taboo.

Vinchenzo, told Ivan "to organise the men into work parties and set up base camp." "Yes sir" replied Ivan and set to work immediately, there was a lot of activity going on in the camp. Peter asked Vinchenzo if he and Marcella could help, "you can start brewing the coffee if you like there are going to be a lot of thirsty guys shortly."

"Ok" replied Peter and turned to Marcella, "come on Marcella you get the wood for the fire and I'll get the provisions out", both men quickly disappeared, as they were sorting out Peter said to Marcella "its good to be helping for a change I've felt so useless this last month."

"Really?" said Marcella "is it a month already I thought we had only been gone a few weeks."

"No" said Peter "it really has been four or five weeks now, its good to be back as a team" Peter said.

"Yes" replied Marcella, "it certainly is."

Peter and Marcella had sorted out and the coffee and were ready, they took the coffee pot and the cups around to the men, the men thanked them and continued to work, it was almost dark and Vinchenzo suggested Ivan should post the necessary guards on the perimeter, he agreed and chose seven men from the work party, they spread out over the whole distance of the camp and disappeared into the jungle, each man was equipped with a high powered rifle with silencer and night vision and infrared night scopes so as to be able to see what was coming towards them.

Time came to shut up shop for the night, Peter was exhausted but nevertheless very satisfied with his days labour, he remembered a piece of scripture he had been taught by his grandmother some years before, from the book of Timothy, in the New Testament of the Bible it said,

"The labourer is worth his wages."
(1Timothy5:18 New.International.Version)

His grandmother always read to him from her Bible, which was always kept by the side of his grandmother's bed, she would fetch it and would tell him marvellous stories of great adventures from it; he liked Jacob best as he always seemed to be in trouble as this was just like him! Always up to mischief of one kind or another, yet always wanting to help others.***

It wasn't long before Peter had fallen asleep, when suddenly Vinchenzo, woke them both, he put his hand over Peters mouth and putting his finger to his lips he motioned Peter to be quiet, Peter froze, Vinchenzo, once again motioned to them to follow him, they quickly rose and followed Vinchenzo, he led them to the river once more and into the boats all the men were in position, one of the guards had seen movement comming towards the camp from the jungle, it was a precautionary measure in case Von Helgar' men had not taken the bait the other evening, Ivan appeared, "its all clear sir, its alpha group heading in."

"Ok men!" said Vinchenzo "help alpha group if they need it, we'll move out in two hours."

Sunrise came up over the canopy of the jungle, Peter thought how beautiful it looked and got the fire going for his morning coffee, just then Vinchenzo appeared, "sorry Peter no time for that now! we must move if we are to reach Brown before Von Helgar does."

Peter said "but!, but I haven't had my coffee yet!"

"Yes I know you haven't" said Vinchenzo "but a mans life may depend on us reaching him in time."

Peter shrugged his shoulders and thought Vinchenzo right, what is a cup of coffee compared to a mans life! then he thought may be there is time for one cup if there is any hot water around, just then he noticed one of the coffee pots had been missed and ran over to it, he lifted it up to feel if there was any coffee left! When Marcella touched him on the shoulder, he flung the coffee pot in the air with fright. Marcella, he exclaimed "that was the last drop of coffee in the camp and its all gone now!"

Marcella smiled "don't worry I've got your daily intake of caffeine in my flask, I knew you wouldn't get up in time so I made you up a flask."

Peter looked at Marcella and said "if you were a woman I'd marry you" and hugged Marcella.

Marcella said "steady on its only coffee."

"Yes" said Peter, "but to me it's life itself first thing in the morning, and in the afternoon and evening he said."

Marcella smiling said "well yes! Peter, I know!"

Then Peter said "but its more important than the other times."

Marcella replied, smiling back at Peter, "your problem is your hooked on caffeine"

"Steady on" said Peter, "I wouldn't go that far."

"Oh wouldn't you" replied Marcella.

Both men burst out laughing, as they headed for the boats, as they approached the boats, Vinchenzo, looked at them, "your happy this morning, what's all that about then he" said.

Both Peter, and Marcella looked at each other and laughed even more, "its ok Father Vinchenzo, you probably wouldn't understand."

The men got on the boat, "let go forw'd" Vinchenzo whispered, the boat drifted out in to the river, the engines fired up and the boat once again headed up river, the other boats in tow. Dawn was braking and the top of the canopy of the jungle began to glisten with shafts of light beginning to break through, the sound of the jungle wakening up was all around them, Peter loved this time of day, and before long the boats headed for shore once more.

Peter asked Vinchenzo, "why they were stopping?"

Vinchenzo replied "we are picking up some guests."

Guests? Peter thought way out here in the jungle! This puzzled Peter, he waited with baited breath to see who these guests were, Peter didn't have long to wait, before long there was a rustling in the trees, just beyond the water line, then from the edge of the tree line two men appeared, Peter couldn't make them out as they were wearing hooded cloaks, they boarded very quietly but quickly.

The boats once again left the shore line and headed up river in the direction of the rising sun, Peter was curious as to whom the men were, this was nagging at him so he went to Marcella, "who do you think they are Marcella?" asked Peter.

Marcella shrugged his shoulders, "I don't know, but I have this feeling whoever they are I should be glad they are on our side."

Peter felt a cold shiver go down his spine, he looked at Marcella, "yes I know what you mean" he said "they are rather mysterious aren't they!"

Vinchenzo came over, "its time you pair got some shut eye, we'll wake you if anything exciting happens", ok replied Peter and Marcella.

Peter said "I suppose you're right I am feeling tired."

The men laid down on the thwarts of the boat trying to get comfortable.

Peter thought to himself, how I would love a nice comfortable bed with fluffy pillows and a nice firm mattress, he smiled to himself and once again thinking, well the sooner we get through this; the sooner I can have my dream come true!

Peter woke suddenly, he wasn't sure why he woke, but he felt something was wrong, he turned towards Marcella, he was missing, where had he gone? The boat was empty, only he remained, where had all the others gone and why had they not woken him? Where were Marcella and Vinchenzo? All these questions ran through his head, and who were those two cloaked; men? Had they overcome Marcella and Vinchenzo in the night? If so why was he left all on his own, then suddenly he was aware of a whistling sound coming from the river bank, out of the trees walked Marcella, "morning Peter" he cheerfully spouted.

Peters mouth opened wide he was so relieved to see Marcella, "where is every body?"

Marcella replied, "Oh they are just ahead of us they'll be back soon don't worry."

Peter sighed with great relief, "you don't know the thoughts that have gone through my head" he said to Marcella.

"Thoughts" Marcella replied "what kind of thoughts?"

Peter said "I thought those two men we picked up last night may have killed everyone!"

Marcella smiled "yes I know what you mean they were rather scary weren't they, beside I didn't wake you because they went on horse back and I knew you wouldn't have fancied that, so I left you sleeping and told Vinchenzo not to worry, I would look after you until they returned", then Marcella said "how about a nice cup of coffee, that should put the world to rights for now."

Peter's face lit up at the thought of coffee, "good idea he said", so Peter and Marcella got out of the boat and started a camp fire and prepared fresh coffee, the aroma could be smelt from far off, it was a rich inviting aroma, the men settled down to enjoy their coffee, when Peter heard voices coming towards them, Peter and Marcella froze, Peter looked towards Marcella and whispered "maybe it's Vinchenzo"

Marcella looked at Peter and said "it can't be they won't be back until this evening", they quickly got up and dowsed the fire, and then they got into the boat, "quickly!" Peter said to Marcella, "let go the rope", Marcella went forw'd and let go of the rope which had been tied around the tree to keep the boat from drifting down river, the boat silently drifted from the shore, Peter directed the boat towards some trees, the boat drifted under the over hanging branches hiding it` from sight of anyone over on the other shore.

The men waited for whoever was coming towards them to appear, they waited with baited breath, Peter and Marcella held tight to the overhanging branches so as not to allow the boat to drift, it seemed to be a long while before Peter could hear the rustling of branches coming from the other side of the river, and the movement of brush, then a man appeared from the trees it was Vinchenzo, "Peter, Marcella, where are you" he shouted! but just as they were about to reply Peter felt something move around his feet, he looked down to see a rather large snake moving across the bottom of the boat, he froze and just stared, the sweat running from his forehead.

"M-m-Marcella" he whispered "it's a s-snake."

Marcella looked down, but by now the snake had filled the bottom of the boat.

Marcella said very quietly "stay still its not bothered about us, its after smaller game."

Vinchenzo was still calling to them, but the men could not answer, Peter was terrified, the snake was about 5 metres long, but to Peter it could have been ten metres or more in length, it came out of nowhere, it never seemed to end in length, it slid along the bottom of the boat, only pausing to lift its head and then proceeding, it finally slid over the side of the boat and into the river were it disappeared.

Peter and Marcella sighed a huge sigh of relief, they pushed the boat out into mid stream again and shouted to Vinchenzo, who had been searching for them down stream, they reached the other bank and tied off the boat, Vinchenzo asked them what had happened and the men began to explain, Peter explained how he had woke up with no body around, he thought something awful had happened, then he heard whistling and then Marcella appeared, "yes, yes" said Vinchenzo rather impatiently, "why were you hiding?." Peter said sorry and began to explain about the voices he heard, voices coming to wards the camp from the jungle, so the men hid in case it was some unwelcome visitors, Marcella chip in, "yes because you said you would not be back until late afternoon we thought it must be someone else."

Vinchenzo looked at the men, "well done he said, its good to know you are both listening and learning, so what took you so long to answer?"

Peter again began to explain, "how just as they were about to reply to Vinchenzo, that an enormous snake entered the boat and began to move over their feet toward the bow."

"It was big said Marcella!"

"Yes" said Peter "it must have been at least 10mtrs in length."

Vinchenzo said "now, now Peter don't exaggerate, the largest snake in this river is 6mtrs"

"Well it was big anyway!" said Peter.

Peter blushed just like a little school boy who had just been caught out by the teacher, exaggerating his tale of adventure, Vinchenzo listened intensely to the unfolding adventure, he waited until they had exhausted themselves telling the story then with a coolness unequalled by anything they had seen before, Vinchenzo said "good now lets have breakfast, and then we can discuss our next move, and explain where we went and why."

Peter went straight to the coffee pot, he and Marcella had brewed earlier, it was still warm thank goodness he thought to himself I need this coffee, he took the old rustic cup he had carried with him since base camp and filled it almost to over flowing, he took a rather large swig and swallowed deeply, it was like petrol to a car engine, it seemed to spring him into life, he was already feeling like a new man, and what had previously happen to him was like a mere nightmare which he had now woken up from and was safe once again.

Vinchenzo called the men over to a space around the fire and in the sand of the riverbank he drew a crude map of sorts, "right as you know we left here early this morning with our two passengers, we proceeded to a reference point previously determined by myself and the two passengers, when we arrived things were not as we expected, hence the reason for our hasty return, as you can imagine things have taken a turn for the worst, we are now running against the clock therefore we must move swiftly and quietly in to action."

Peter asked "what happened?" he then looked at Vinchenzo and said, "I know! I know! Be patient all will be revealed in time."

Vinchenzo smiled at Peter, "not this time Peter, we arrived at the designated target and found some of Von Helgar' men laying around; there had been some sort of incursion and Brown was nowhere to be seen. So we must assume that Von Helgar has Brown, and if so this is most unfortunate as we believe Brown to be in possession of the map, now we don't know how long Brown will be able to hold out against Von Helgar' methods of extracting information, but my guess is not long."

The men all agreed that time was of the essence, Vinchenzo continued, "now we know that Von Helgar has a base at the foot of the great waterfalls about three days forced march from here, he will go there first, but won't stay there long as he will know we would have found the camp by now, whether he will have realised we found the hidden bodies of his men, or not! He will probably have to assume we have, therefore he will head for his base camp in East Germany. He'll take Brown there before interrogating him, so we must make preparations for the next leg of our journey gentlemen and that is Eastern Germany."

Vinchenzo continued, "Hindrich go back and get the jet prepared, Ivan, Franz go and pay a visit to Von Helgar' camp and take our two esteemed guest with you, Michael and the rest of you stay with me."

The men got up and each prepared for their respective operations, Peter and Marcella, both got ready, they packed their stuff together and headed for the boats.

Vinchenzo turned to Ivan and Franz and said "we will wait four days for you then we will leave, if you don't make it, join us as soon as you can at the usual place."

"Very well sir" the men replied, then Franz asked "how thorough would you like us to be sir?"

Vinchenzo looked at Franz, and Ivan and said "as thorough as you can be in this case, use extreme prejudice in all matters pertaining to this mission, it is time Von Helgar was taught a long over due lesson!"

"We understand sir, extreme prejudice it is!"

The men left, disappearing in to the interior of the densely, over grown jungle.

Vinchenzo turned towards the boat and motioned to the few men left that they should leave now, Peter and Marcella picked up their gear, which they had barely unpacked and headed towards the boat.

Peter looked at Marcella and whispered "here we go again."

The boat once again drift into mid stream, but this time they were heading down river not up and the long journey to East Germany, as they began to move down river Peter noticed a large log type object in the river it seemed to be moving towards them, Vinchenzo had noticed it too, he took the riffle and took careful aim he fired one volley the crack of the shot sent hundreds of birds fluttering and chirping above the canopy of the jungle, the object in the water rolled and disappeared beneath the murky waters of the Amazon.

Peter looked at Vinchenzo and asked "what it was he was shooting at?"

Vinchenzo leaned forward and picked up a rather large boat hook and leaning over the edge of the boat he hooked what looked like the log, as he raised the hook towards the boat, Peter could see a head appear; that of a rather large snake.

Peter said "wait a minute that looks like the one that entered our boat!"

Vinchenzo looked at Peter and Marcella "are you sure he said, all these reptiles look a like to me!"

Both men nodded and said "yes, It definitely looks like it to us."

Vinchenzo said "then God was truly with you, this is an anacondas it's a boa constrictor it eats its prey whole and that has sometimes been known to have been of human origin!"

Peter swallowed sharply as he thought what might have happened!

Vinchenzo laughed "its alright Peter this one wasn't big enough to swallow a man whole even though they can become that large, no this one was just seeking some nourishment a monkey perhaps or small rodent that would get too close to the shore line, I shot him for food they make good eating out here the natives swear by them and we can trade it skin for information about Von Helgar."

Peter sighed with relief as did Marcella at the thought the snake was dead and they were finally heading back to civilisation once more.

The men reached base camp once more, Peter was glad he could finally stretch and change his clothes, but first he thought a good swim in the river to cool off would help greatly, the boat touched the river bank and Peter got out, he secured the bow line, the men entered the camp it was in a bit of a state; the surprises Ivan had left most certainly worked, the men got down to work to clear away the mess; Peter, was just about to head for the water, when Vinchenzo suggested "that if Peter was thinking of bathing in the river he should reconsider."

Peter looked up and asked "why?"

Vinchenzo looked towards Michael, Michael nodded and took a piece of raw meat that came from the uncooked snake and walked towards the river, Vinchenzo followed as did Peter and Marcella, as Michael approached the river bank, he threw the meat into the water, Peter and Marcella watched as a long line of bubbles headed for the direction of the meat now floating near the surface, then suddenly there was a hive of frenzied activity and the meat was gone, Peter cringed, "that's why you shouldn't go swimming, Tiger fish they can strip a man to the bone in minutes, it's a painful way to go said Vinchenzo."

Peter gulped and said "fine! Ok, I can live with that", then turned and walked away muttering to himself, well how was I to know that there are some crazy fish in the river?

Vinchenzo suggest "that they should eat a good hearty meal as they had a long arduous journey ahead of them the next day, and that a good night's sleep for all would do them the world of good as they prepared to move out early that next morning."

Peter and Marcella sat by the open fire, Peter with his large rustic coffee cup steaming from the hot coffee he had just filled it with, he and Marcella were going over that days events and talking about the run in with the snake. They could see the funny side of it now, and both men just laughed, Peter suddenly went silent, Marcella asked him "what was wrong?"

Peter replied "I nearly went swimming, I could have died!"

Marcella reassured Peter that was not the case as long as Vinchenzo was around, "Vinchenzo knows everything" said Marcella "we are in good hands!"

Peter smiled and said "I know, but I still worry."

"Yes I know what you mean", replied Marcella, then said "well enough of that tripe we are still here and that's all that counts right now, so lets go to bed and worry about tomorrow when it comes!"

Peter nodded and the men retired, to their resting places, Michael was walking about still and this made Peter feel a little more secure knowing that Michael would be around all night.

Peter lay down on his blanket and looking in to the starry heavens reach into his rucksack, he fumbled around until he took hold of a small Bible that he carried with him; it was one that his grandmother had insisted he carried with him always! And as a good grandson he had done so, Peter got out his torch and opened the bible, he had opened it at the book of Isaiah and chapter 41: he read the words, "fear not for I the Lord your God am with you, I will hold you up with my righteous right hand."

Peter closed the Bible and dwelt on those words of comfort, slowly he drifted off to sleep, in the reassurance that God would protect him.

The next morning Peter rose to the smell of the coffee on the open fire about ten feet away from him, he opened his eyes he could see Marcella crouching down near the fire, Marcella turned and smiling said "good morning sleepy head time to rise and shine" he said to Peter.

Peter threw back the blanket and got up, he headed straight for the smell of the coffee, Marcella already had his favourite cup filled with the hot coffee, Peter took hold of the cup in both hands, and began to sip at the black hot liquid, and just then Vinchenzo appeared and said "we leave in one hour!"

Peter looked relieved, and said to Marcella, "oh good I thought he was going to say right lets be having you then we've got to go, I don't think I could take another rush start before at least five cups of coffee!"

Marcella looked at Peter and shook his head, he began to laugh, "come on Peter I'll fill your cup up again" and picking up the coffee pot leaned towards Peter, Peter held out his cup eagerly, and Marcella poured, he and Peter began to laugh at the situation and even Vinchenzo and the others saw the funny side to this conversation.

The men packed up camp and left in the boats, it was about a day's journey to their pickup point and they would reassemble at the airfield, where they would rendezvous with Ivan and the others.

As they travelled down river Peter, thought about all that had happened over the past few months, how one moment he was enjoying life in Rome, and here he was now heading down the Golden Condor stretch of the Amazon river, back to an airfield just outside of Brasilia the capital of Brazil, to fly to an unknown place in Eastern Germany! Then he thought to himself "well at least its no-longer separated by the Berlin Wall, and it is Europe!"

Peter suddenly became aware that Marcella was speaking to him; he had been so involved in his own thoughts that he had become oblivious to the others around him.

"Look Peter" Marcella exclaimed, pointing to the shoreline "it's a crocodile! look at the size of it; it must be as long as that snake we saw!"

Peter was hoping to put that episode behind him, but was to be starkly reminded of this by Marcella, the crocodile was a big one Vinchenzo was on the bow of the boat with his riffle ready to shoot the crocodile if it came to close to the boat, they were often known to capsize small boats and eat the occupants, this of course was purely a precautionary measure.

The boat ran the current around the bend of the river, from there they could see the jetty where they would alight from the boat, there was a man standing at the jetty waiting for them as they approached, Vinchenzo jumped onto the jetty and he and the man hugged as if long lost friends, Peter took the bow rope and tied it around the bollard on the Jetty, then walked towards Vinchenzo.

Peter stopped short of them and staggered, it looked like Angus, the man they had killed he thought to himself, Vinchenzo looked at Peter and Marcella and introduced the man.

Peter, Marcella, he said "this is the real Father Angus!" the men looked astonished, Peter said "but he looks just like the other man, you know the one we had to", Peter suddenly stopped in his tracks and thought what if he doesn't know yet.

Father Angus spoke "its alright Peter, he said I already know about Angus junior, Vinchenzo informed me, and I know it had to be, he had gotten greedy for the riches of man."

The men left in the waiting vehicles and arrived back at the airfield, as they arrived Peter could see Ivan and Franz they had only just arrived back from the looks of them and had sustained casualties, they were bringing the wounded off the choppers as they were arriving.

Vinchenzo went over to Ivan and Franz, they seemed to be getting a debrief as they were walking together, Vinchenzo patted both men in a well done gesture, then he returned to the others, "right lets go he said! And get straight on to the jet."

The men got out of the vehicles and started to walk towards the plane, once on board, Peter asked Vinchenzo if "everything was alright."

Vinchenzo looked at Peter and said "Peter sometimes in battles men are hurt, we suffered some minor casualties but believe you me Von Helgar suffered far more", then he smiled in a reassuring way and went towards the cockpit, he turned back for a second and said "thank you Peter the men appreciate your concern for them, now fasten your seat belts we'll be leaving in a short while."

The plane taxied once more and the adventure continued as they soared into the heavens, they were off again! Peter thought to himself as he watched the ground disappearing below, I wonder what adventures lay ahead this time, it may not be snakes and crocodiles but he was sure it was going to be fraught with danger and excitement.

Peter laid back and closed his eyes once more, and dreamt of work in the Vatican Vaults and how safe he felt there, and his cosy flat and lovely warm comfortable bed.

It had been some hours later, when Peter woke up, he was still rather drowsy, he looked towards faithful Marcella who had got Peter a nice fresh cup of his favourite coffee, this was always a welcome sight to Peter and Marcella knew just how he liked it, he took hold of the cup and sipped at it lovingly, he smiled at Marcella and said "thank you" in a soft quiet voice.

Marcella replied "you're welcome", and sat back down with a cup of coffee of his own.

Peter then asked Marcella "how much longer before we land do you think?"

Marcella said "Vinchenzo had informed him that, we would be there in an hour or so and that was a bout half an hour ago, so I shouldn't think we'll be long now."

Just then Vinchenzo' voice came over the intercom system, and told them "to fasten their seat belts as they were coming in to land."

The men straightened themselves up fastened their seat belts and prepared to land, the plane suddenly started to turn and reduce altitude, the plane once again hit the tarmac of the runway and the plane came to a gentle halt, Peter and Marcella unbuckled their seat belts and exited the plane, they walked towards a dingy looking shed style building.

The building was grey and cold looking, it was the most unwelcoming place Peter had ever seen, this was even more dingy than the castle they had been held captive in when they were in Russia, and that was saying something Peter thought to himself.

CHAPTER 6
Beyond the Mountains Edge

They had landed just outside of Leipzig, in Eastern Germany, at a long forgotten airfield used by the Luftwaffe, in the Second World War, it looked like it hadn't been used for some time, it was just a hut in a field or so it would seem.

As the men approached the hut, a woman appeared from nowhere, she approached Vinchenzo, she saluted and said "all the preparation are ready sir just as you requested."

"Very good" replied Vinchenzo walking briskly towards the hut, Peter looked at Marcella "she's a woman!" he said in a surprised voice."

"Yes" replied Marcella, "I think she's called a female member of staff."

Peter realising how stupid he must have sounded quickly shut up, Marcella just smiled and shook his head at Peter, Peter felt embarrassed as he realised the woman heard what he had said.

When they arrived at the hut Vinchenzo opened the door and they entered into a what only could be described as a common room, probably used by the pilots as a place to congregate while wait for something to happen, like a squadron scramble.

Vinchenzo and Ivan entered a smaller room off to the side, the woman followed; the others stayed in the larger communal room, a short while later the three returned to where the others were waiting,

Vinchenzo began the meeting by introducing Peter and Marcella to the female member of staff.

"This is Annette", he said, "she is our operative in Eastern Germany, she is Hindrich' daughter! She is our eye's and ears on the ground here, she will now brief us on Von Helgar' movements since he returned yesterday, Annette please if you don't mind!"

Annette, stepped forward, "thank you sir", Annette began, by saying "now pay attention! Von Helgar, arrived yesterday at 1500 hours, he landed approximately 20 kilometres from here:", she turned and pointed to a map and a small town just outside of Leipzig, then turning back to face the men she continued "he and his men unloaded what looked like a coffin, we believe this held Brown, they loaded it on to a waiting truck and proceeded east to this castle! The location of which cannot be approached by air or road, however, it lies on the edge of a lake which Von Helgar considers un-breach able therefore, he only has one lookout tower on its perimeter, and we have already entered the castle this way without arousing suspicion so we have scheduled a mission to go in seventy two hours", she paused for a moment then began again "now you may be saying why seventy two hours? Annette again paused! "Well because it's the only night that is moonless, you see if there is a moon we would be visible on approach; this way we will be hidden from sight by the darkness that falls on a moonless night around here."

Annette continued "We will go in two waves, the first wave will be led by myself, the second by Franz, we will first take out the guard on the tower which over looks our point of entry!"

She looked up to where Carl and Hans were sitting, Carl she said "if you and Hans can take out the guards as well as you dealt with them in Russia?"

Carl and Han's looked at each other, smiling they both nodded and said "our pleasure we assure you!"

"Good" replied Annette, "now the likelihood is they wont know what has hit them until it is too late, and may I remind you gentlemen no hostile prisoners if you please!"

Vinchenzo stood up and thanked Annette, then turned and asked, "Right any questions?" but as usual with the usual thoroughness all had been accounted for and no one spoke.

Vinchenzo then said "good I now suggest we get a good nights sleep for we have a long day ahead of us tomorrow, Peter you and Marcella join us in the other room will you."

Peter and Marcella nodded, the men rose from the comfortable chairs they had managed to grab before everyone else, and head towards the open door of the other room.

"Come in" said Vinchenzo, "now tomorrow, Peter, I want you and Marcella, to go into Leipzig, to this address, there you will join up with Hindrich, and two other men, you will then leave Leipzig on the 1615 express train for Bonn, there you will go to Father Angus' and telephone Monsignor O'Connell at the Vatican and tell him that the research is going well is that clear."

Peter nodded and replied "Yes got that."

Vinchenzo continued with what he was saying, "now tell him also that we should have a result shortly, then hang up the phone and leave by the rear entrance of the building, once outside head back to the train station."

Peter and Marcella once again nodded their approval, Vinchenzo once again continued, "once there you will find in the lost property office a parcel for Jenkins just ask the attendant for it he will find it for you. Once you have the parcel open it up, inside will be three sets of clothes change into them, in the right hand pocket of one set of clothes, you will find a key go to the left luggage locker and place the key into the lock, but do not open the locker straight away wait 10 seconds and then open it!"

Peter looked at Vinchenzo with a puzzled look on his face, then asked Vinchenzo, "Why ten seconds?"

Vinchenzo said "you'll see soon enough, please Peter just trust me", said Vinchenzo.

Peter looked at Marcella who just shrugged his shoulders; well Peter said "aren't you even remotely curious?"

Marcella said "no! that's your department I think, so why should I be?"

Peter looked amazed and thought to himself, am I the only one around here who is even remotely curious about this mission, perhaps I need some coffee! That's it he thought, that's the answer I am in caffeine withdraw, no one else seems to question anything any more, and that worries me! he thought to himself, Peter agreed.

Vinchenzo, looking at Peter, said "are you sure you are alright with the way things are going?"

Peter replied "yes! Yes, I'm sure."

Peter mumbled under his breath once more, why ask me, no one ever tells me anything anyway, its always wait and see, wait and bloody see! I'm fed up with waiting, why can't they just trust me!.

Vinchenzo carried on, "now when you open the locker and retrieve the contents, which is a small holdall type carrier, head for the train and return here as quickly as possible, on your return bring the holdall straight to Ivan then report back to me, is that clear?"

Marcella replied "yes we understand!"

Peter was silent for a moment, "re you sure your alright Peter?" Vinchenzo asked

Peter suddenly looked up towards Vinchenzo, "yes"; he paused for a moment before answering again, "yes! I'm just tired."

"Yes" replied Vinchenzo "we all are! Its been a long day for us all, so let us all go and get a good nights sleep!"

All agreed and they left the room, leaving Vinchenzo and Annette to finalize the plan and hopefully tie up any loose ends.

Peter and Marcella, placed their sleeping rolls against the back wall, Peter then headed for the coffee pot and poured the piping hot liquid into his favourite mug the rustic one, although sometimes Marcella was sure it wasn't so much rustic as rusty, but Peter loved that old mug and if it kept him happy thought Marcella what harm could it do.   .

Peter walked back over to where Marcella lay on his bed roll, "would you like a cup of coffee Marcella?" he asked.

"No thank you Peter" replied Marcella, "too late at night for me I'm afraid."

Peter sat down on his bed roll, still thinking about that snake and how scared he felt as it moved over his boots, but then, he thought how tasty it was when cooked, this surprised Peter as he had never tasted snake before, he just smiled to himself and thought ha! Who ate whom, in the end?

Peter drank his coffee and unrolled his bed mat then curled up and went to sleep, dreaming of a wonderful feather bed and a warm room.

The next morning Peter woke once again to a flurry of action, he turned to look at Marcella, but he was already up and getting Peter, his life line, his first of several cups of coffee, "come on Peter get up", said Marcella "we are due to leave for the station in half an hour! And you haven't even had your first cup of coffee yet!"

"What! What time is it for goodness sake?" Peter said in a startled way.

"what time is it" replied Marcella, "It's almost ten o'clock time you were up and ready to leave for the station."

"Well why didn't some one wake me earlier?" replied Peter!.

Marcella just mumbled, "we did", but, you were dead to the world! he thought.

Peter said "what was that?"

Marcella just said "this coffee's a bit hot I'll give it a swirl."

Peter looked at Marcella in a disbelieving way, "oh, yes I'll bet you did!" both men started to laugh and Peter drank his coffee, he thought oh yes I can now face the day ahead! that first cup always tasted the best and how he clung to the cup, it would have taken a surgeon to separate Peter from that cup.

Vinchenzo entered the room, "good morning Peter, good morning Marcella I hope you slept well?"

"Yes thank you" replied the men!.

Vinchenzo, began by saying, "well its time you two were off, now remember your instructions and good hunting."

"Thank you" replied both men.

Vinchenzo said, "Your transport to the station awaits you outside so lets get a move on eh!"

Peter quickly got ready and he and Marcella headed out of the door to the awaiting vehicle, the journey to the station took almost an hour, as they were travelling along, Peters mind began to wonder, as he thought of all that had happened to him and Marcella over the past few months. Once again he reflected on how it all started that fateful morning when Angelo walked into the office they were working in and placed that piece of scroll onto Marcella' desk at the request of Marcella after Vinchenzo had asked Angelo to take it to Marcella, Marcella had been working at the photocopying machine and was too busy to take the piece of parchment from Angelo. Peter remembered the first time they realised that this was no ordinary piece of parchment, the excitement he felt and his eagerness to pursue the matter, he remembered vividly how when those men held a gun at Marcella' head and how he had been so afraid that they were going to kill him. Suddenly the car pulled up outside of the railway station, they were there, Peter was a bit bemused, as he realised that they had arrived, where had the time gone, he thought to himself, they had been travelling almost an hour and it only seemed to be a fleeting moment in time to him.

Both men got out of the vehicle, then quickly walked towards the platform display boards to find out the time of departure of their train, Marcella quickly obtained the necessary information, then turned to Peter and said "come on Peter we are leaving from platform 1 in five minutes! So we've not much time"

Peter picked up a news paper and headed with Marcella towards the platform and the awaiting train, they boarded the train and settled down for the short journey into Leipzig. Once again Peter looked out of the window of the train, his mind full with questions like why am I here? What will happen next? What's in the holdall at the station? And who the hell is Monsignor O'Connell?

It wasn't long before they arrived in Leipzig at 11:01 and headed for the address they had been given, the men got into the taxi and showed the address to the driver, the driver turned around and said "are you sure you want me to take you here?"

"Yes please" replied Peter, we are absolutely sure, peter sat back and in a low voice said "I think!"

Marcella asked the driver why he had asked them if they were sure they wanted to go there, the driver replied "well I know it's none of my business but I wouldn't want to go there, it's a rough area of Leipzig!"

Marcella thanked him for his advice but assured him that's were they wanted to go, the driver said "that's ok then if you're sure!" And drove off in the direction of the address.

Peter and Marcella arrived at the designated address, they got out of the taxi and knocked at the door, while the men waited for an answer, Peter looked around and momentarily thought to himself, hmm, the driver was right it looks rough around here!.

Peter noticed a group of people walking towards them, one of the men had a knife in his hand, it was quite clearly in view, another had his hands in his pocket as if holding a weapon of sorts, just then, the door opened and Hindrich appeared, he looked up towards the approaching men, the approaching men stopped for a moment, Hindrich wavered to the men and they returned to what they were doing as if Hindrich had some sort of hold over them.

The men entered the dingy building and into a room where they sat at a large round table, "ok" said Hindrich "we stay here until we leave for the station in two hours, so make yourself comfortable gentlemen."

Hindrich, got up and went into the kitchen he was only gone a short while when he returned with a coffee pot and three mugs, Peters face lit up! As he smelt the aroma of the coffee, "I thought this would cheer you up Peter" said Hindrich, because the whole camp knew Peter was partial to a cup or two of the old crushed coffee bean!

Peter looked at Hindrich, and said "well its true I suppose I do like the odd cup now and then, the men began to laugh together as Peter realised what he had said and how ridiculous it sounded.

Back at the airfield Vinchenzo and the others were preparing for the assault on Von Helgar' stronghold Carl was preparing the cyanide quarrels for the cross bow and Ivan and Si were getting the plan of attack down to a fine art, everyone knew their job and place, Annette, was going over the final details of the incursion, when a man arrived at the field, he immediately called Vinchenzo over, Vinchenzo and the man walked and talked for about twenty minutes, Vinchenzo listened intensely as the man spoke: his body language told Annette all was not well.

The man returned to the car and left again, Vinchenzo headed once more for the hut, he said to Annette "call the others over we need to talk, quickly he said!"

"Yes sir" replied Annette and left to fetch the others.

Vinchenzo sat and waited, as he did so he thought I must get a message to Hindrich, I'll send Si, he should get to Leipzig station in time to catch the others leaving for Bonn, just then the others came in, Vinchenzo said "thank you for joining me so quickly gentlemen and lady there has been a development. It would seem that Von Helgar has found out about our presence and is sending a taskforce to intercept us, we only have hours before they will arrive."

"Now then" Vinchenzo continued, "Si head for the station and connect up with Hindrich, inform him of the situation and then new rendezvous point, which will be at point delta."

"Very good sir" Si replied and left immediately.

Right Vinchenzo began ""Ivan, Annette, I want some pretty nasty surprises for our unexpected guest."

"Very well sir", Ivan and Annette looked at another smiling, then they too left the room.

Vinchenzo carried on "Carl I think its time you had some moving target practice of the extreme kind don't you?"

Carl smiled and said "yes I think you may be right sir" and he left also.

Vinchenzo said to the rest of the men, "ok gentlemen time to pack up and leave", everyone nodded and left the room.

Si, reached the station and waited for the next train in to Leipzig, as he boarded the train, he noticed two men getting on the train a couple of compartments down, Si, thought to himself those men seemed familiar? Then he remembered that he had been on a mission once and these two men had been there also, they were Von Helgar' men, two of his elite, notoriously brutal assassins, Si, waited to see what they would do next, the train moved out of the station and arrived in Leipzig some thirty five minutes later, Si, headed for the train notice boards and looked for the platform at which the Bonn train would leave from, the two men were still in tow, just then Si caught a glimpse of Peter, Marcella and Hindrich, he walked towards them and brushing past Hindrich he looked at him and indicated with his head for Hindrich to look over his shoulder, Hindrich looked at Si, and then quickly over his shoulder, he turned back and nodded to Si in an approving way, the men headed for the train and boarded immediately, Hindrich and spoke very quietly to Si, and Si walked further along the train entering a compartment some three compartments away from where the others were sitting, just then two men dressed in long black leather coats boarded the train and took up residency in the compartment next to Si, the whistle for the train to move away from the station sounded and the train moved off slowly at first, but then picked up speed rather quickly.

Hindrich sat near the door of the compartment and waited, the train entered a long tunnel; this was approximately a half hour into the journey, all Peter could see was the lights of the train glimmering on the wall of the tunnel as it moved along, Peter was suddenly aware that Hindrich was missing, he wondered where he had disappeared to, then he thought he must have gone for a leak, just then the door opened and Hindrich and Si walked in, "where were you?" Peter asked.

"Oh just taking in the fresh air and scenery."

Scenery! Fresh air! thought Peter we were in a tunnel what scenery? What scenery, what fresh air? Oh well he thought best not ask.

Si was holding his side, "are you alright?" Marcella asked Si, just then Si keeled over he had been hurt, Marcella, quickly undid his coat and opened his shirt it was a knife wound and a severe one at that, Marcella was trained in first aid, but this looked too serious and may be beyond even his capabilities he thought, he said to Peter "go quickly and bring some water in whatever you can, I must stop this bleeding!"

Peter rose and fetched as much water as he could carry, he returned to find Si had died the wound was as Marcella thought too severe for Marcella to have done anything.

Hindrich opened the train window and leant Si against it, he lifted Si' legs and pushed, Peter was astounded, "wh-what are you doing?"

Hindrich explained the situation to the two men and said that "if Von Helgar' men found Si, on the train dead and his two assassins not on the train he would suspect that we had taken care of them, however, if they found neither Si, nor his assassins on the train he would merely think they had missed that particular train and were waiting for the next train, that will give us valuable time, we now need all the help we can get!"

Peter looked at Marcella and "said this is getting dangerous!"

Marcella looked at Peter and said "It's a bit later to say that now isn't it look lets just trust in Hindrich' judgment and go along with it."

Peter replied "yes well as you've put it like that I suppose your right."

The train pulled in at Bonn, the men alighted and headed for the taxi rank, "taxi" shouted Peter!

Hindrich said to Peter "no need to hail a taxi Peter we'll take this one", a vehicle stood in the corner of the railway station, it didn't look much like a taxi thought Peter, the men approached the car, Hindrich took some keys from his pocket and opened the car door "get in gentlemen!" he said, the men got in and they drove off in an Easterly direction, it wasn't long before they arrived at a block of flats near the University, the car pulled up at the rear of the building and the men got out, Hindrich then got back in to the car, then said "you know what you have to do! now go quickly and do it!"

The men entered the building and headed for Angus' room as they approached the room they noticed the room the door was slightly ajar, they quietly approached and opened the door and very carefully, (they had learnt a lot since the beginning of their adventure), they pushed the door open slowly to reveal furniture strooned over a vast distance, someone had really given the place a good going over, however, the flat was empty, whoever had been here was long gone, Peter picked up the phone and using the number Vinchenzo had given him he rang Monsignor O'Connell, the phone rang for a while then a voice at the other end said "hello Monsignor O'Connell speaking, how may I help you?"

Peter repeated the message Vinchenzo had given him and put the phone down, The voice on the other end of the phone replied "I understand, relay to Father Vinchenzo my congratulations on a job well done."

The phone then went dead. The men quickly left the flat and headed to the rear entrance of the building, they got back into the waiting car; Hindrich asked "if all was well?"

Peter told Hindrich what they had found on entering the flat and the telephone conversation with the voice on the other end of the phone.

Hindrich, said "we had better leave in case they were watching the building!"

Slowly and almost noiselessly Hindrich moved off, they head for the station once more and the lost property office, on arrival Peter went in and asked for a package for Jenkins, the man left Peter and retuned with a brown paper wrap, Peter gave the man the ticket that Vinchenzo had given to him before they left and proceed to the gents where Marcella and Hindrich were waiting for him.

The men quickly changed their clothes and headed for the locker , the key for the locker was in Marcella' pocket, Marcella took the key out and search for the locker with the corresponding number, they quickly found the locker and placed the key in the lock, he was about to turn the key, when he remembered Vinchenzo words wait ten second before turning the key, it echoed through his mind, he waited and then turned the key in the lock, suddenly what sounded like a intermittent tune could be heard then a clunk and the door opened, inside was a holdall, just like Vinchenzo said, however on the back of the door was a small canister, this was linked to the locking system, now he understood why Vinchenzo wanted him to wait ten seconds, the canister had cyanide written on it, if he hadn't waited ten seconds they would have all died.

Marcella grabbed the holdall and the men headed for the train back to Leipzig, the train was just about to pull out, the men boarded quickly and the train moved off out of the station at Bonn , Peter turned to Hindrich and said "well that went smooth enough."

Hindrich looked at Peter and said "we are not out of the woods yet!"

"What do you mean?" asked Marcella.

Hindrich asked "Peter and Marcella if they had noticed the two gentlemen that had rushed to catch the train?"

Peter said "yes but I thought they were just late, and besides they weren't wearing long black coats!"

Hindrich smiled and said "you are still a bit naive yet aren't you Peter, not all of Von Helgar' men wear long black leather coats."

Marcella said "so you think they are Von Helgar' men then?"

"Yes I'm sure" replied Hindrich! "One of the men I recognise."

"How do you know him" replied Peter

"It's a long story" said Hindrich "but he is my half brother!"

Peter stood amazed, "your brother he said?"

"Half brother!" replied Hindrich.

Marcella said "its funny, you can pick your friends, but not your family!"

Peter apologised to Hindrich, Hindrich smiled and said "you weren't to know Peter, just as you could not have known Si was Annette' brother and my Son!"

Peter felt helpless he didn't have the words to comfort Hindrich, he felt so helpless, he really wanted to give Hindrich a big hug and say kind words of comfort to him, but he knew at this stage that would only make things worse, the train journey had taken an hour up to now, they were about half way, when Hindrich said "come on its time to leave!"

Peter thought leave! Leave and go where? There are no more stops between here and Leipzig" or at least none he was aware of.

Hindrich, whispered to Marcella " we must get off before the train stops, or else there will be a reception party waiting for us, now Peter may be a problem but leave we must!"

Marcella looked at Hindrich and said in a very quiet voice "leave Peter to me he trust me", Hindrich agreed.

Marcella tugged at Peters clothes "come on Peter" he said!

Peter reluctantly rose "where are we going?"

"Come on you'll soon find out", Marcella said.

The men entered the corridor and headed for the luggage car, they arrived at the door of the luggage car, Hindrich, and Marcella knew if they told Peter what they were about to do he would freak out and that would alert Von Helgar' men, that was unacceptable in both of their views, so the plan was as they approached their drop off point they would open the door of the train and push Peter out, thereby avoiding any unnecessary commotion.

The time came for the men to leave the train, Peter was asking allsorts of questions like why are we here and not in the comfortable compartment? when suddenly Marcella threw open the carriage door and pushed Peter towards the open door, Peter, who before he knew what was happening, had left the train and was now hurtling towards the embankment of the railway lines, Marcella quickly followed and Hindrich shortly afterwards, the men rolled down the embankment, where they were met by two other men, "are you alright sir?"

"Yes! Yes I'm alright! how is Peter?"

Marcella ran over to where Peter was, "are you alright Peter?"

Peter lay their stunned; he looked up at Marcella and said "I think I need a cup of coffee!"

Marcella laughed "he's alright" he said, he took Peter by the hand and helped him to his feet, Marcella looked at Peter and began to apologise to him, Peter just raised his hand in a gesture to Marcella, and replied "its ok Marcella, I'm glad you didn't tell me what was going to happen, because if you did I wouldn't have!"

Peter headed with Marcella to where Hindrich and the others were waiting; the men got in to an awaiting vehicle and headed to where they would meet the others, in the car Peter said to "Hindrich just one question?"

Hindrich replied "of course Peter anything!"

"Why are we not going to the airfield?"

Hindrich told Peter what Si had told him, how Von Helgar had found out, how they were just outside Leipzig and how he was planning to attack them so the camp relocated to point delta, leaving a few surprises for Von Helgar' men in the process, Peter smiled, "yes I can imagine he said!."

The men arrived at the main camp where Vinchenzo, was waiting for them to arrive, "did everything go well? Is Si, not with you?" He asked.

Vinchenzo was particularly fond of Si, so it came as a blow when Hindrich told Vinchenzo what had taken place on the outward journey of the train to Bonn.

Vinchenzo told Peter and Marcella to freshen up before supper and then he would explain what was in the pipeline for tonight, they both left Vinchenzo and Hindrich to talk, just then they saw Annette heading towards Vinchenzo and Hindrich, she fell on Hindrich' neck and they hugged in a sombre way.

Evening came and all were gathered in the main tent for supper, they ate a hearty meal and then sat down to business, Vinchenzo began by apologising and explaining how they had lost Si, the room fell silent a sombre mood fell over the room, Vinchenzo said a prayer and a few words about the loss of Si, Si was well liked by all and would be sorely missed, then Vinchenzo began the meeting by saying "now! down to business gentlemen and lady of course, even though we see Annette as one of us and not her gender, we've had to move operation strong bow up by twenty four hours because of circumstances of late, so we go in tonight just after twenty three hundred (11 o'clock)."

Vinchenzo continued, "this means we won't have the cover of darkness we would have liked it's a partial moon tonight therefore the shimmer off the lake will leave us with some exposure so quick the word and silent the attack, I'll hand over to Fran's, and Annette, now for your final instruction and all that's left to say is good luck and good hunting!"

"Franz said now gentlemen I suggest you all get ready for your part in the operation, and to the guards be extra vigilant to night until we return just in case Von Helgar and his men decide to counter attack."

Everyone left the tent except Peter and Marcella, Peter was hovering around a fresh pot of coffee like a bee around a honey pot, Marcella asked him if he was alright?

Peter turned and smiled "yes! yes, I'm fine thanks, its just the thought of leaving that train as I did, I'm so grateful you didn't tell me!"

"That's alright Peter, we knew if we told you, you would have froze and probably injured yourself on landing, this way you didn't have time to realise what was happening!"

Peter turned to Marcella and said "Marcella, you have to promise me that if anything goes wrong this evening, you wont let them take me alive?"

Marcella looked shocked and was stunned at what Peter had said, Peter was always the brave optimistic one between them, Marcella replied "nothing will go wrong I promise Peter."

Peter paused and looking once again at Marcella he said "promise me you won't let them take me alive please?"

"Ok" said Marcella "if that's what you want then I promise."

"No!" Peter said "I want you to say it, and mean it! that you won't let them take me alive?"

Marcella looked at Peter, his face was almost angelic, Marcella said "I Promise I won't allow them to take you alive!"

Peter smiled at Marcella and said "thank you" in a sheepish voice and carried on drinking his coffee, it wasn't long before Ivan appeared, "are you ready to leave he asked?"

Marcella looked at Ivan, "yes we are ready" he said.

"Good then lets roll" replied Ivan!.

The men went outside to the waiting transport and climbed in, the Lorries left in single file, and it took two hours to reach the embarkation point.

When they arrived they got out and began final preparations for the assault on Von Helgar' stronghold, Peter and Marcella watched as the men prepared, then Vinchenzo came over to them "right Peter, Marcella go with Carl and stay out of sight until we give you the signal, the rest of you know what to do, now lets get moving we have only one hour to get into position so lets move it!", he said and everyone headed for their positions.

The men arrived at their designate positions after a half hour trek, Carl took up his point of reference as to give himself the best possible shot at the sentry on guard duty, then he waited for the moment when he would execute his orders, he looked at his watch, and took aim, there was a dull sound and a whooshing noise as the arrow left the bow and in what seem a fleeting moment the arrow reached its target.

Peter could see the silhouette of the man fall, there was barely a sound and the man was down, Carl gave the signal to Vinchenzo, Vinchenzo signalled Ivan, and Annette, who immediately took up their positions and headed towards the wall of the castle. The operation to rescue, Brown was underway. The team under Annette's command moved into the shadows of the overhanging rock and began to climb the cliff, followed closely by Franz and his unit, they breached the wall on time and began to spread out over the parapet.

Annette looked down into the court yard, she could see men moving around below, she signalled to a couple of men who quickly and quietly headed for a tower and then disappeared into the darkness, Annette, then she signalled to a third man with a cross bow who took aim and fired, the arrow flew in the direction of a man in a tower across the court yard, it seemed to hit him and he fell down.

He then he re loaded the cross bow and once again took aim, he fired once more and another guard fell, then Annette signalled the rest of the men to go into action, Peter could hear gun fire from were he Carl and Marcella were waiting, Vinchenzo signal the men that were left including them to move forward, as they did Vinchenzo ran to the bottom of the cliff, the rest of the men followed and started towards the top, they had caught the garrison asleep, they entered the castle to find that Von Helgar had already left.

By the time Vinchenzo and the others arrived the fracas was almost over; what resistance remained was soon over run and the search began for the map and Brown, Vinchenzo asked Franz "how many casualties they had sustained?"

Franz reported "three dead and several wounded."

Vinchenzo, asked "who the dead were?"

Fran's informed him "Petrov, Anderson and Chan!"

Vinchenzo said, "Make sure they are buried with full military honours."

Franz replied "of course sir" and disappeared into the courtyard, Vinchenzo went over to Annette and asked, "are we secure?" he said.

Annette replied "we are sir."

"Good" Vinchenzo said, "now is Von Helgar here?"

"Negative sir he and a small expedition left a couple of hours a go."

"Did they take Brown do you know?"

"Negative on that sir, we are looking for him now."

Just then; a man appeared from the direction of a large tower, he came up to Vinchenzo and spoke softly to him, "I've found a body sir in the dungeon."

"Do we know who it is?" said Vinchenzo.

"We are not sure sir."

"Right" said Vinchenzo "lets go and have a look! shall we"

The men headed for the direction of the tower, Peter, Carl and Marcella quickly followed. The men entered the tower, there was a spiralling stair case going down they reached the bottom it was a long dark passageway with only one dull light to light their way, it opened up to a large cavern style cave, which had what only could be described as medieval torture equipment on the walls and there in the corner was what looked like a pile of rags.

Vinchenzo approached the heap in the corner, it was a body! Or what was left of it, "Von Helgar' men had most certainly surpassed their brutality this time" said Vinchenzo; it indeed was Brown he had been skinned alive.

Vinchenzo stood there silent as if he was saying a prayer over Brown, then he turned and said "was there any survivors to the conquest?"

The man with them said "not as far as we know sir, all of Von Helgar' men were dead, from the looks of things, approximately one hundred and fifty men in all." "Right!" Vinchenzo said, as he turned and headed up the corridor.

He told the man "to tell the rest to meet him in the courtyard of the castle as soon as possible!"

The man replied "yes sir" and ran ahead of them by the time Peter, Vinchenzo, Carl and Marcella arrived in the courtyard everyone was assembled, "ok listen up!" Vinchenzo said "I want this castle searched from top to bottom; to try to ascertain where Von Helgar is headed is that clear!"

"Sir yes sir" came the reply and everyone hurried off, just then two men dragging what looked like another man appeared, from the direct of the far corner of the courtyard, One of the men began to say, "this one is still alive sir, we found him clutching this piece of paper."

"Good bring him here."

The man looked at Vinchenzo "I'll tell you nothing he said!"

Vinchenzo looked down at him, smiling "ho I think you will" he said, then turned to the men and said "take him to the dungeon and I'll be there shortly."

The men dragged the other man towards the tower, "wait, wait" he yelled!

Vinchenzo turned, bring him back here!" he said.

The men turned and dragged him back to where Vinchenzo was waiting; "well" Vinchenzo said "where is Von Helgar?"

The man replied "he left a couple of hours ago, with the map; and said he was heading for the eagles nest! that's all I know I promise you."

Vinchenzo smiled and said reassuringly "I'm sure your right", then drew his revolver and shot the man in the head, Peter was lost for words, Vinchenzo had taken another mans life without flinching! he had never seen this side of Father Vinchenzo before and this worried Peter, Peter looked at Vinchenzo in a condescending way and asked "was that necessary?"

Vinchenzo looked at Peter and said "oh yes, very necessary, this man is responsible for that mess you seen down in the dungeon!" Peter swallowed sharply and hung his head in shame for doubting Vinchenzo, Vinchenzo looked at Peter and said "its ok Peter you are allowed to question."

Peter just looked at Vinchenzo and said "sorry I doubted you.".

Vinchenzo called the rest of the teams together, "come on he said we must move and quickly, Von Helgar has a three hour start on us by now and he's heading for the eagles nest, and that's beyond the mountains so lets get a move on!"

Everyone jumped into the vehicles left in the castle and headed for their vehicles that were waiting a kilometre away, there they would transfer to their own wagons and head after Von Helgar.

The men arrived at the dispersal point and transferred to the other vehicles, then journeyed on towards the mountains, Peter asked Vinchenzo "where they were going and was it far?"

"Yes its is I'm afraid Peter, it will take us the rest of the night and part of tomorrow to reach our destination", Vinchenzo continued, "it is imperative that we reach the eagles nest by noon, Von Helgar is now in full possession of the map and we must retrieve it before he reaches the valley beyond the gateway."

"The what?" Peter asked, just then Marcella took hold of Peters arm "enough questions Peter we'll find out soon enough!"

Peter looked at Marcella in disgust but then paused for a moment and thought well, perhaps Marcella is right "if I don't know what's a head of us then I won't worry." Peter again looked at Marcella and said "ok, perhaps you're right!"

"Good man" said Ivan.

But Peter's sense of curiosity was chomping at the bit he wanted to have the whole thing laid out for him on a silver platter, talking of which he thought I wonder if Angus knows that his cleaner is crap!

And had anybody told him about his flat? then he thought well perhaps its better he finds out himself.

Vinchenzo still had the holdall with him; Peter thought I wonder what's in that holdall? It never felt heavy so what is it? Perhaps it's a new secret weapon! Or some new fan dangled piece of equipment, yet to be tested!

Once again Peter's imagination ran rampant with curiosity; Vinchenzo took out a map and was studying it when he opened the holdall and took out from it what looked like a polythene sheet which had markings all over.

he took the polythene sheet and placed it over the map, Vinchenzo then began to show Ivan something, he reached once more into the holdall, pulling out yet another sheet and placed that over the already covered map, this puzzled Peter as he tried to peer over towards the map, Vinchenzo and Ivan laughed, "come on" Vinchenzo said to Peter "your minds curiosity must be getting the better of you now."

Peter blushed! He moved closer to see what the men were doing, Peter could see that the two pieces of polythene sheets were lining up with certain points, not that he could understand what this mean's, so to save his embarrassment he said "oh! that's what you've been doing."

Peter said, then he said "I feel quite sleepy now so I shall leave you two gentlemen to get on with whatever you were doing and say good night."

The men smiled "that's alright then, good night Peter" they said, and he moved back to his seat, it was a rather bumpy ride Peter thought to himself but he must get some shuteye.

Peter woke up to the sound of rattling weapons at his feet he sat up to see they had reached the mountains, the lorries were struggling against the steep up hill gradient of the mountain pass, the wagons slowed down to a crawl then they turned off onto an even more bouncy track, they carried on up the mountain side groaning and rattling as they went, Peter looked over to Marcella who was just stirring into life, "rough ride isn't it?" he said.

"Sure is!" said Marcella, who was almost wide awake by now. Vinchenzo and Ivan were still in that same position as when Peter went back to his place to sleep, just then the wagons came to a halt and Vinchenzo and Ivan alighted the vehicle, Peter could hear voices outside but couldn't make out what they were saying then Vinchenzo popped his head around the tailgate of the vehicle "sorry! Men we get out here and head up on foot: the road a head is block with a landslide!"

The men got up and vacated the vehicles, the road was narrow and the drop steep, Peter clung to the wagon for grim death, slipping by on to the wider road that lay in front of the wagons, the men assembled on the road and prepared to continue their journey on foot, it took about four hours walking to reach the point of their destination, Peter was worn out, "we'll rest here!" said Vinchenzo, then he took Franz, and Annette to one side Peter was trying to hear what was said but couldn't get close enough without arousing suspicion, just then Vinchenzo came over to Peter and Marcella and said, "we'll move out in an hour so get as much rest as you can, when we move out I want you two to stay close to Carl, alright!"

"Yes Father Vinchenzo" Peter replied.

"Good then rest now", Vinchenzo said.

Peter lay back against a rock and was admiring the view when Marcella came over to him and said "coffee Peter?"

"Oh' yes please" replied Peter, he took the cup of coffee which Marcella had made for him in his favourite mug and savoured the flavour and the view which was quiet spectacular he thought, Peter could see for miles either way across the undulating hills and the vast expanse of the valley, he thought this is as close to heaven as I'll ever get I suppose.

Time was up and the men prepared to move off, they split into three groups and went off up the mountain in ten minute intervals, Peter and Marcella were in the last group with Carl, Vinchenzo and Ivan were with Franz in the second group, where as Hindrich and Angus, were in the first group with Annette, they would rendezvous at the eagles nest in two hours. The teams arrived at the rendezvous point, Annette had already established a strong hold, Franz and Ivan, were probing to find out if Von Helgar had already arrived, when Peter, Marcella and Carl arrived.

Peter asked Carl "what was happening?"

Carl said "I'm not sure but I'll ask if you like?"

Peter replied "yes please; if you don't mind."

Carl answered "I don't mind at all Peter", and walked over to Vinchenzo.

The men spoke for a while and then Carl returned to where Peter and Marcella, were waiting, he told Peter and Marcella, that they should stay where they were, so that the team's could secured the area and make it safe, Peter and Marcella nodded in acceptance of the situation.

Two men approached Vinchenzo, and said "sir we found the entrance, it looks like it has very recently been used, we found a number of foot prints around the entrance, shall we go in sir?"

"Yes very well but use extreme caution as you are aware Von Helgar is a very dangerous physco-pathological killer, who will stop at nothing to obtain the map that will lead him to the gateway of the garden, we must stop him at all cost and retrieve the map!"

"Yes sir" the men replied.

Vinchenzo, called Annette and Ivan, over to him, "go with them" he said "and take Alpha and Bravo sections with you, that will leave me with Charlie and Delta sections to secure our position until we hear from you."

"Very well sir" replied Annette and off they went in the direction of the entrance, then Vinchenzo turned and headed to where Peter and Marcella were sitting by a large rock formation, Peter had already started his second cup of coffee, Marcella had seen to that as he had carried about six pounds of it in his kit for Peter, Vinchenzo approached the men, "well how's things going?" he said.

Peter looked up "they'll be much better in about ten minutes." Vinchenzo and Marcella looked at each other and Marcella motioned noiselessly with his mouth the word coffee, Vinchenzo smiled and said, "I know what you mean, that coffee's going to do wonders for us all, Peter looked up "well if we are all going to benefit from my coffee, I'd better make some fresh then hadn't I?"

As up to now Peter had been filling his mug up from his and Marcella's flask's, Peter thought well I had better get the fire going hadn't I!

Both men started to laugh then Vinchenzo said, "yes Peter you had better!"

Marcella' head just shook and hung down as he laughed in amazement, he thought to himself it would be easier to turn this mountain upside down than to separate Peter from his coffee.

Vinchenzo sat down beside them and said "now look Peter, things are going to get decidedly rougher before long!"

Peter looked at Vinchenzo he could see by the look on his face that this was serious, Vinchenzo continued "from now on in, I'm assigning Carl to you as your personal bodyguard, he will look after you as well as Marcella, please do everything he say's without question this is important, your very life depends on it!"

Peter swallowed sharply, replying "of course; whatever you say Father Vinchenzo." Vinchenzo replied "good" however, I do feel you can drop the Father bit while we are in the field as it were."

Peter, looked at Vinchenzo and said "ok, if you insist", Peter had a rare smile on his face as if to say I'll try but no promises, after all he had been Father Vinchenzo to Peter for a long time.

Vinchenzo looked at Peter, and replied, "well at least try!", Peter smiled once again, Vinchenzo smiled saying "then I'll leave it at that for the moment." Vinchenzo got up and went over to where Father Angus was.

"Angus old friend" he said.

Angus turned, "yes Vini" he replied.

"I need you to return to Rome immediately and inform O'Connell what's happening, once you have done that return to Point Zero and await further instruction."

"Very well Vini, perhaps on the way to Point Zero I can call in on my old friend Hamish Mctaggat and perhaps he'll allow me to take a service or two as well?"

Vinchenzo smiled, "yes and give the old goat my blessings when you see him!"

Angus laughed in his hearty way, "I most certainly will and I know he'll appreciate it."

Angus and two other men picked up their gear and headed down the mountain.

Peter had his coffee gripped tightly in his hands, he was thinking about what Vinchenzo had said to him, it must be important for me to listen to what Carl tells me?, because Vinchenzo has never looked so intense as that moment when he looked me square in the eye, he thought, and his voice was deadly serious he thought!, just then Angus came over on his way down the mountain to say good bye and that he hoped they would meet again some day.

Angus said "if they were ever in Bonn they would always be made welcome."

The men thanked Father Angus then Peter said to Marcella in a very quiet voice, "only if he gets a better house keeper and sniggered."

Ten as Angus walked on he shouted back "I will Peter, I will!"

Peter almost spilt his coffee in surprise, Marcella began to shake his head and laugh, Peter said "surely he can't have heard what I said, could he?"

Marcella said "just drink your coffee Peter!."

Vinchenzo was speaking to Annette on the radio then he said "ok lets move out." Peter was stunned he had just made three fresh pots of coffee this was truly sacrilege he thought to himself, three pots of coffee wasted! just then some of the men came over and started filling their water flask with the hot coffee, one of the men winked at Peter "thank you he said it gets rather cold in these caverns, and this will warm us up nicely."

Peter stopped and thought for a moment, that's a cracking idea he though so he emptied his water flask and refilled it with coffee, he got up, picked up his kit and headed to where Carl and Marcella were waiting.

Marcella looked at Peter and said "you ready?"

"Yes I'm ready" Peter said.

Marcella noticed Peter was looking rather smug, he asked Peter "why he was looking so pleased with him self?"

Peter replied "oh well you know", as he patted his water flask.

Marcella looked at Peter and said "well that didn't take you long to cotton on too, did it."

Peter smiled and replied "no! not at all."

Vinchenzo led the way down a winding narrow path that led to a croft of trees, just beyond the trees lay an entrance to a cave the men approached it with extreme caution just in case it was a trap, they entered in two's.

As they entered, they scanned the area before Vinchenzo an the rest entered, once inside they lit the place up with powerful torches the likes Peter had never seen, so small yet so powerful.

Annette appeared from out of nowhere she immediately went over to Vinchenzo, "report Annette" he said.

She immediately began to explain their position and how they had engaged some of Von Helgar' men in combat.

Vinchenzo asked "if there were any casualties?"

Annette replied "one wounded sir, but its only a flesh wound, six of Von Helgar' men dead."

Vinchenzo paused for a moment, then he spoke and said "that means he has only two men left with him, of course that assuming he has no extra men spread along the way."

Annette spoke, "looks like it sir and he can't be far a head."

"Ok" said Vinchenzo "keep probing."

Annette disappeared as quickly as she had appeared into the dark shadows of the cave.

"Come on" said Vinchenzo "we must move on and quickly!"

The men proceeded down a long corridor of rock it twisted and turned in all direction, until they came to a cross section, it split into three ways, straight ahead, off to the left and an opening to the right, Peter thought, I hope Vinchenzo, takes the right route!

Vinchenzo, told one of the men to check for a direction marker of some sort that either Franz or Annette would have left, the man checked all three entrances, he then returned to Vinchenzo and pointer to the left, Vinchenzo signalled to move to the left, as they moved off Peter wondered "how they knew which way to go?"

As they passed the entrance of the cave to the left, Peter notice a cross on the wall, he smiled as he remember his grandmother used to say to him Peter always follow the way of the Cross, they had been going about two or three hours; when once again Annette appeared she said "sir we found an entrance and it looks like someone has recently opened it up and left by way of it."

"Von Helgar do you think?" asked Vinchenzo.

"Possibly sir" replied Annette.

Vinchenzo asked Annette to show him, they went down a passage way. They were gone some time when suddenly they returned, Vinchenzo said "right lets go! the eagle has flown the nest, we must move quickly!"

Everyone was up on their feet and in moments the group were heading on down the passageway, in which Vinchenzo and Annette had appeared.

The group reached the exit, Peter and the others had to cover their eyes as the bright sunlight hit them as they emerged from the cave entrance, Vinchenzo ordered the choppers in to lift them from the ledge, as this would save time and buy them a couple of days worth of catching up with Von Helgar.

Peter, looked at the view; it really was breath taking, then he thought to himself, a couple of hours rest and a pot of coffee would go well here, then Carl approached Vinchenzo and whispered something in his ear, Vinchenzo nodded in an approving way and Carl returned to the cave entrance disappearing into the darkness once more, to reappear some twenty minutes later with a large black holdall, it must have been with Von Helgar' men.

Carl took it to Vinchenzo who laid it on the ground and slowly, very slowly opened it, it contained a rather large what looked like explosive device, made up of depleted uranium, they were probably to use this as a last resort if they thought they were going to be over run.

However. Annette had caught them totally by surprise, that's probably why they never used it, Vinchenzo called over Enricho one of the taskforce members who was ex bomb disposal and an expert in his field, Vinchenzo told him to take the bomb and make it safe to travel.

"Yes sir" the man replied "will do", he took the package and retired to a safe distance, he opened the holdall and taking out a small wrap of tool from his vest began to work on the device, it seemed to take an age, but finally the man returned to Vinchenzo, "it's safe sir!"

"Good" replied Vinchenzo, just then came the sound of a rushing wind! swirling rotor blades appeared, "good! here's the choppers said Vinchenzo, "every body get ready to move."

Then four helicopters rose from the valley floor, they couldn't land because of the narrowness of the ledge, so the hovered as close to the edge as possible, the men got into the choppers, as each one filled so it moved away from the edge of the overhang and the next one moved in, when it came to Peters turn he froze with fear so Marcella took hold of Peter's arm and "said come on Peter you can do this!"

Peter looked at Marcella and in a sheepish voice said "can I! can I really?"

"Yes Peter you can!" said Marcella, Marcella tried to reassured him, Peter took a deep breath and flung himself on to the helicopter, he hit its hard metal deck with a thud, Peter opened one eye "am I still alive?" he asked, as he opened one eye and looking up realised, he'd landed at Vinchenzo feet, "yes Peter you are" said Vinchenzo "now up you get and put your safety belt on we don't want you to fall out now, do we eh!"

"No! not at all" Peter said and quickly got up and sat in the seat next to Marcella who had got on in all the commotion.

Peter quickly brushed himself down and asked Vinchenzo where they were off to now?"

"You'll see" he said, "you'll see!"

The helicopters returned them to the airfield, where the jet was fuelled and ready for take off; Vinchenzo gave Annette a hug and kissed her on the cheek, then Hindrich, came over and walked a while with Annette, after a while Annette turned and hugged Hindrich as if she may never see him again and kissed him, then everyone but Annette and her section boarded the aircraft, Annette waved as the jet took off, Peter wanted to know where to but no one was saying least of all Vinchenzo, this worried Peter things seemed to be intensifying of late, Peter lay back n his seat looking out of the window, Peter loved the window seat he could watch the clouds flitter by and the scenery on the ground especially if they crossed the mountain tops as they were doing, Peter soon fell asleep and was woken to his favourite smell, that of freshly made coffee, Peter looked out of the window but all he could see was snow, snow for as far as the eye could see, "where are we he asked?"

"Over Alaska I think" said Marcella.

"How long was I asleep?" asked Peter.

"Oh three or four hours I think."

"That long eh", said Peter "well it didn't feel like that long he said smiling."

Vinchenzo came in and said "we'll be landing shortly so buckle up."

Peter asked Vinchenzo "where they were going to land? as all he could see was snow and no sign of civilisation!"

Vinchenzo smiled "you'll see Peter, soon enough, you'll see!" he said, then headed back for the cockpit, Peter glanced once more out of the window, suddenly there appeared a speck on the horizon, it slowly grew and grew as they got closer, it was a large settlement barely visible from the air let alone from the ground, the jet circled, then from what seemed to be coming from below the surface of the ice, a set of lights appeared just like a runway, the plain descended and came to a halt just outside of the settlement, the men got up and headed for the huts on the outskirts of the settlement, Peter noticed the Inuit population here were, strangely dressed, he felt something was oddly familiar about this place but he couldn't quiet put his finger on it.

CHAPTER 7
The Serpents Head

Vinchenzo and the men assembled in a large hut at the edge of the settlement, Vinchenzo began by asking "Ivan and Franz to go to check out the situation so far as the readiness of the men were?", they nodded and left, Vinchenzo continued to say "Hindrich you go and find out if there is any news yet concerning Von Helgar."

Hindrich replied "right sir!" and left by the rear entrance, then Vinchenzo pulled out the map from the small holdall that Peter and Marcella had retrieved for him from the station in Bonn, a few days earlier, he laid the map out on the table and said "gather round men", everyone squeezed around the long table.

Vinchenzo began to explain the situation to everyone, just then a tall grey haired man entered the room, he approached Vinchenzo and lent towards his ear, he spoke softly, Vinchenzo looked up and said "you will have to excuse me for a moment gentlemen: something has come up which requires my immediate attention."

The men around the table stood bolt upright and saluted as Vinchenzo and the grey haired man left the building.

Peter was almost squashed to death when the men stood up straight, his breath seemed to be squashed out of his body in one swift movement, when Vinchenzo had gone the men relaxed and Peter sighed with relief and took in great mouthfuls of air, he headed straight for the smell of the freshly brewed coffee on the stove, he thought to himself someone must have known he was in need of such sustenance.

Vinchenzo return a short while later and resumed his talk, he explained that "Von Helgar, was on his way to a place not far from where they were!", he pointed to a position on the map called the serpents pass, the said "here lay the entrance to the "Gate", this "Gate", was the starting point at which one needed to be to start the journey to the lost "Garden of Eden" however, first one must pass certain test and feats of bravery before they could arrive at the gate, this fascinated Peter, feats and tests! he thought, I like puzzles he thought, Peter was a fairly well accomplished chess player, he loved games that stretched the mind, even more so when it involved tasks of some sort or other, he wondered if Vinchenzo would allow him to do the necessary, when it came to passing through to the "Gate".

Suddenly! Peter, was aware of Vinchenzo explaining what would happen if they got it wrong, Peter listened intently, Vinchenzo began by saying, "first off at the beginning of the trials you get two chances, but as you progress this diminishes, and no mistakes are allow, if you fail any part of the test you will be evaporated, in other words you will just disappear and no one has ever returned from failing the test of the pass alive so we don't even know if we can get back once we are committed, therefore knowing this I have decided that only essential personnel will go on any further Ivan."

Ivan looked up at Vinchenzo and said "yes sir!"

"Dismiss any men with wives and families only single men may go and no more than one from a family."

"Very well sir" Ivan, replied, the men left the table and as they did Peter thought oh well that's that then I'm bound to be left behind as I'm the weakest link here, he slowly and dejectedly walked towards the coffee pot, then he thought to himself no! I'm not going! I want to stay, I've come this far and I'm not given up now, I'll go and talk to Vinchenzo.

Peter turned and headed for Vinchenzo "now look here Father Vinchenzo, I'm not given up now, I'm no child you know; that you have to wrap up in tissue paper, no! I'm determined to carry on no matter what the cost."

Vinchenzo looked at Peter astonished at his eagerness, and boldness, "of course your going Peter we need you more than you'll ever know."

Peter continued "and if you think you can scare me!" Peter paused, realising what Vinchenzo had said "what! You mean I can go?"

"Yes Peter you must go."

Peter almost squeezed the breath out of Vinchenzo as he hugged him, then he ran over to Marcella like an excited child on Christmas morning, "I'm going he said!, I'm going yippee."

Marcella smiled "calm down Peter, calm down" Marcella said, "here have a cup of coffee."

Peter slowly calmed down, then reality of the situation hit him, he thought what did Vinchenzo mean I was the most important factor in this expedition? then he thought oh well as long as I am going I'm sure all will be revealed.

Ivan assembled the men that were to go home, he wished them well, then Vinchenzo appeared and said it had been a great privilege to have served with them and hoped they would serve together again in the future, but for now their mission was complete only a chosen few could go on, the men cheered Vinchenzo, and then dispersed, those that were left, were called into the cabin once more.

Vinchenzo, began to explain once again the problems that lay ahead, even Vinchenzo had never gotten this far before, they had always retrieved the map before it got this far, however they had not face such a formidable and determined enemy like Von Helgar before either, this troubled Vinchenzo, it perplexed him how Von Helgar, was receiving so much inside information!, he was always ahead of the game it would seem, Vinchenzo, thought long and hard over this matter, then it struck him, he realised what was bothering him, may be Von Helgar was a rouse of some kind after all no one had ever seen Von Helgar, not even him, he was always a phantom figure in the background, what if! he thought to himself, Von Helgar was one of his own people? What if, that was how he always knew what they would do next?.

These thoughts encapsulated his mind, he would soon find out, he would set a trap, but he would tell none else, not even Fran's his most trusted colleague, he must be as wise as the serpent himself on this occasion.

The men formulated the next move, they would leave in a few days, after the men had rested and gained their strength they would need all the strength they could muster if they were to flush out Von Helgar, "it's time for supper I think" suggested Ivan, Vinchenzo agreed and the men left the building.

Vinchenzo said to Peter "stay close to Carl and Marcella."

"Ok" said Peter, then the men entered a house, just beyond the edge of the settlement, "this is where we will stay" said Carl, a small plum ply built woman appeared from around a curtain, hanging near the rear of the house, she saw Carl and ran up to him, she hugged him as if she thought she had lost him, then a man appeared an elderly chap obviously native to the surrounding area, his face was weather worn yet friendly, Carl introduced Peter and Marcella, then turning to them he said "this Maria and Lopez, my adopted parents, whenever we stay here it is always with Maria she is the best cook for hundreds of miles around."

Peter and Marcella felt humbled, then Peter smelt the freshly made coffee he headed straight for the direction of the aroma, he grabbed his favourite cup from inside his wrap and began to pour, Maria and Lopez, looked at each other in a bemused way, Marcella tried to explain to Maria and Lopez "that Peter was a caffeine addict", they just laughed, "yes, Carl, warned us earlier, that's why we had the coffee ready, we though Carl was exaggerating but obviously not", they laughed again.

Peter looked around, he was totally oblivious to what had just happened then carried on drinking.

Peter headed for the blazing fire that burned in the huge fire place, now this was bliss he thought to himself, this I can live with!

Maria came over to him, "would you like more coffee Peter?"

"Oh yes please if that's alright."

"Yes" she said as she went to fetch him another cup, "we have several pounds in the store I think that should last you a couple of days."

Peter was stunned "I'm not that bad! am I he asked?"

Everyone just laughed, "take no notice of Maria" said Lopez "she has a wonderfully dry sense of humour."

Peter shrunk in the chair, muttering to himself; I love my coffee but some people would have others think I can't live without coffee, but I'll show them, I'll cut down just to prove to them I can go with out coffee, then he thought I sincerely hope I won't have to do it for long, maybe just a day or two, I'll show them! And he once again supped on his wonderful cup of coffee, then they all retired to a good nights sleep.

Time at the settlement went all too fast for Vinchenzo and the men, they had no sooner arrived than they seemed to be off again, however, they had appreciated the rest and the wonderful hospitality they always seem to receive from the people, Vinchenzo and the others had often stayed There over the years and were always made to feel welcome.

Vinchenzo called the small group together, there was only a dozen of them now besides Vinchenzo, he made the thirteenth member of the group, there was Peter, Marcella, Carl, Ivan, Hindrich, and several other hand picked men, Vinchenzo said "they would set off on sledges until the glacier, then it would be a trek on foot, to the foot of the great falls, then the climb up to the serpents pass before they would have to face the "tests of time" as they were known."

This was the part Peter was looking forward to, it would be his chance to prove his worth to the men, he would be no longer a spectator rather a participator, if only Vinchenzo would allow him to volunteer, he would have the chance to pester Vinchenzo on the way.

Peter was sure, he could wear Vinchenzo down given the chance, he was desperate to do this no matter the what the cost, it was all or nothing now for Peter, he felt his time had come and he had no intention of letting anyone or anything stand in his way.

The party loaded up the sledges, three in all, and prepared to leave, Vinchenzo, would ride in the first sledge, with Peter in the second and, Marcella in the rear sledge, it would take them two days to reach the glacier, and it would be cold.

At night they would make camp only travelling in the daylight, as at night the temperatures plummeted, to such an extent nothing living could survive, it would freeze a mans blood solid, only Polar Bears and Ice as far as the eye could see.

Vinchenzo motioned the sledge train to move off, the villagers waved a fond farewell and once again they were on the move.

Vinchenzo headed North, by North East, the sledges slowly moved off, it wasn't long before the settlement had vanished into the distance, Vinchenzo checked his compass then sat back in the sledge he covered himself in the warmth of the seal skin wrap that had been provided this was to keep out the cold, the dogs howled as they ran along. They had been travelling for quite some time, when suddenly they stopped the men had gotten off the sledges and were gathered together a short distance away. Vinchenzo soon joined them, as did Carl and Ivan. Peter had popped his head out from the warmth of the sealskin and was now wondering what was going on, he left the warmth of the sledge and walked towards the men, as he arrived he saw that they were examining some sort of tracks, he approached Vinchenzo, "what's going on he said?"

Vinchenzo said to Peter, "oh nothing just some fresh animal tracks, if we are lucky we'll catch up with it and have fresh meat tonight for supper, now back to the sledge because we must push on he said."

Peter headed back to the sledge and opened up the sealskin compartment, he climbed in and waited, it was about ten minutes later that the sledge finally began to move, the dogs howled once more as they strained to pull the sledge, it seemed an age to Peter before they stopped again, this time it was for the night.

Peter once again opened up the sealskin canopy and peered out, "right Peter you and Marcella help Carl to set up the tents! Meanwhile both myself and Ivan, will set up a perimeter around the camp."

Peter rose to the occasion, helping put up his own tent and that of Hindrich', Vinchenzo was impressed, "well done Peter he said keep up the good work."

Peter then set about making coffee for everyone, Peter enjoyed being useful, as he had felt for a long time that he was more of a hindrance than a help, he took a cup of coffee to everyone and even made sure the dogs had some food, Peter liked dogs and they seemed to like Peter, he stroked the dogs and then returned to the now erected tents, inside the tent he and Marcella, had erected for themselves, Peter had a boiling hot pot of coffee on the go, this would be a welcome sight to anyone in this weather.

He climbed into the tent and settled down, the wind had picked up it was now rattling the sides of the tent, Peter just sat there with his cup of coffee, he didn't care what it was like out there he was snug as a bug in a rug where he was.

The wind howled most of the night, Marcella struggled to keep warm mainly because Peter had swung himself around in the tent, next morning Marcella was up and around early he had lit the camping stove in their tent and was brewing up hot coffee, as soon as the aroma hit

Peter's senses he began to stir in his sleeping bag, Peter opened his eyes, "morning Marcella."

Marcella smiled "good morning Peter, how are you? I trust you slept well?"

Peter replied "I'm good, and yes I slept well thank you, and how are you this morning?" Asked Peter.

"Yes I'm good" he said, "would you like coffee Peter?" Marcella asked.

"Mm that would be nice, yes please" replied Peter.

Vinchenzo popped his head through the tent opening, "morning Marcella, morning Peter we leave in half an hour ok!"

"Ok" they replied "we'll be ready."

"Good" Vinchenzo said and left the two of them to get on with what they were doing. Carl stood outside as Vinchenzo approached, "morning Carl."

"Morning sir, I would think Peters awake with the smell of that coffee!"

Vinchenzo smiled, "yes he does like his caffeine I must admit", the men walked along together discussing the day ahead, Vinchenzo, remarked that one of the sledge dogs was rather poorly during the night, and that Carl should look after the dog until they could replace it or it recovers sufficiently to go on, "stick it with Peter in his sledge, he seems to have an affinity with these dogs."

"and if it should die sir?" said Carl.

Vinchenzo looked at Carl well, "we'll cross that bridge when we come to it, however, we may need it for food if we get stretched."

"Yes sir" said Carl "I understand!"

Vinchenzo then said "not a word to the others, if they ask, we are just giving the dog a rest."

"Very well sir" and at that Peter and Marcella emerged from their tent, "right lads" said Ivan "pack your tents neatly away and stow them on the sledge, Marcella join me in my sledge, Peter you've got a passenger with you."

Peter looked puzzled for a moment then he opened the snug canopy of the sledge to reveal one of the sledge dogs, Peter made a fuss of it straightaway, the dog licked Peter all over his face, Peter laughed, "it tickled" he said,

Carl looked at Peter and said "I think he likes you."

Peter replied "yes I think your right", then he got inside the seal skin canopy with the dog, the other men loaded up and they were off again across the snow once again, it was around midday when Peter popped his head out from underneath the canopy of seal pelts sewn together to make a protective wrap over the sledge, he could see the mountainous ice wall ahead, they drew nearer to it with every passing minute.

Peter quickly stuck his head back in the sledge and the warmth of the canopy, the dog was recovering quite well now, it seemed to have gained its second wind, so he thought that he should let the others know as soon as they stopped! This would allow the dog to return to its duties, helping the other dogs to pull the sled, this would alleviate some of the pressure on the other dog's work loads

The time soon flew by and they came to a halt, Peter popped his head out once more, they had reached the glacier, and in record time according to Vinchenzo, this was truly good news for the men, for if they had been longer and predicted then the weather would have been against them,

Carl looked pleased; as did Vinchenzo, "come Peter, see the glacier."

Peter walked over to were Vinchenzo was standing, Peter said, "isn't it beautiful." The men gazed at the wonderful kaleidoscope of colour that came shimmering down as the sun in all of its majestical glory shone upon it, the ice reflected the light into a mass of different colours, it was like being inside a rainbow, Vinchenzo turned and said "come along we leave the sledges here, Peter how's the dog?"

Peter looked at Vinchenzo "fine" he said "much happier now."

"Good" said Vinchenzo, "we won't have to eat it after all and laughed."

Peter, shuddered when Vinchenzo said those words, he looked at Marcella and Carl and said "he wouldn't would he?" They both smiled and reassured Peter that the dog was safe, Peter sighed a sigh of relief, then followed the other two to fetch his kit, the men moved off quickly wasting no time, they began their assent to the top of the glassier, the climb took some time, but eventually they came to a ledge, right said Vinchenzo, "we'll camp here for the night, Peter stay with Carl and Marcella they know what to do."

Carl told Peter to "dig out the ice in the wall, making a cave so as to sleep in."

Peter asked why did he have to dig a cave in the ice?"

Carl explained to Peter why and said "this would help to keep them warmer and safer in-case of an avalanche in the night."

Peter, did as he was told and the men got the camp stove working, they brewed up immediately, as the climb had been hard and the chill factor high, they snuggled together for body warmth, and settled down for the night.

Morning seemed to come very quickly, Vinchenzo was already up by the time Peter woke up, as were the other men, Vinchenzo was planning the rest of the assent, he had calculated that it would take them the rest of the day to reach the summit, so they had to make tracks as quickly as possible, Peter, got out of his sleeping bag and headed straight for the coffee pot, he got out his favourite mug and began to pour the hot coffee into it, the aroma of the coffee quickly brought Peter to his senses, he sipped at the hot coffee savouring every sip.

Once Peter, was sufficiently awake he rolled up his sleeping bag and put it in his rucksack. Then the men were off again, it was a difficult climb but the men eventually made the summit, not without the odd piece of excitement though, Peter had been on a ledge when it gave way, he fell about ten feet before Carl had managed to secure the rope around a grapple he had hammered into the ice moments before. Peter was hanging there; some two hundred feet in the air, the men quickly pulled Peter to safety, but not without loss, Peters favourite mug had managed to fall out of his rucksack and plummeted to the valley floor below.

Peter was very upset at this but then thought, at least it wasn't him who fell to his death, and besides the mug could be replaced whereas his life couldn't, at least he thought so anyway.

The men rested at the top of the glacier and once again preparing for a harsh tundra night in their tents, Peter missed his old faithful mug when it came to coffee time, but Marcella was carrying a spare with him, Peter thought this isn't as good as my own mug but it filled the need very well.

The next morning the men set off across the vast waste of the snow covered glacier, the cold was biting in now even more than before, Peters fingers and toes felt numb nevertheless, he was determined to carry on, Vinchenzo came over to him, "are you alright Peter? He asked."

Peter looked at him, "yes" he replied "a bit cold but otherwise alright."

"Good!" said Vinchenzo "not far now until we reach the outskirts of the snow valley."

"Where exactly are we?" said Peter Vinchenzo just smiled and again repeated, "not far Peter, from where we need to be, keep going and we'll soon be there."

Peter looked around him all he could see was snow, an endless vast snow field, which seemed to have no end to it, they carried on until they reached a cave in the ice, Vinchenzo held up his hand and said "stop!" everyone stopped, Peter though to himself we must be stopping for something to eat and a lovely hot cup of coffee, so he took off his pack and laid it in the snow then sat on it, he was so grateful for the rest that he didn't hear Vinchenzo tell them to move on, Marcella went over to Peter and asked him "if he was alright?."

"Yes" replied Peter.

"Good" said Marcella "we are going into the cave come along."

"what!" said Peter "but I thought we had stop to have lunch or something!"

"No" replied Marcella, "we are moving into the cave, now come along!"

Peter pulled his weary bones up once more and thought oh well the coffee was a nice thought anyway, the men entered the cave and walked for what seemed ages, Peter was suddenly aware that the feeling was returning to his hands and feet, the burning sensation was now starting to get to Peter, he was also starting to perspire under his thick warm sealskin overcoat, Peter began to wonder if he was sick or something, when he noticed Vinchenzo and the others taking their overcoats off, he thought he was hallucinating so he rubbed his eyes, but it was true, up ahead Peter could see daylight, it was bright, the men emerged into what one could only describe as a tropical paradise, Peter was amazed, where did this come from he thought to himself, then Peter threw off his sealskin overcoat that had kept him so warm over the past days, he looked over towards Vinchenzo who had already undressed and was now in short selves and basking in the heat, "come on men" said Vinchenzo "we've still a long way to go."

Peter was still looking around, he marvelled at the sudden and dramatic change in events, one moment he was freezing cold, wondering if he was going to survive; and now here he was in this wonderful tropical heat, it was like being back in Brazil, then a shiver came over him as he thought to himself of the incident with the rather large reptile (snake).

Peter was now aware that his toes were hurting him far more now, Peter looked towards Vinchenzo and asked "can we stop just for a short while."

Vinchenzo came over to Peter, "what is it Peter? He asked! Peter, answered "its my feet they're burning."

Vinchenzo told Peter to sit down on the rock near to him, he then called over Ivan, Ivan he said, "Peter has a problem with his feet, can you do anything for him?"

"I'll have a look sir" said Ivan, and at that he took out his knife and cut up the laces of Peters boots, he carefully opened the sides of the boots and as gently as he could he took the boots off, the relief on Peters face was amazing, then he pulled down Peters socks, this was far more painful, this revealed that Peter had suffered frost bite but it wasn't as bad a case as Ivan had seen, however, the toes on Peters right foot had started to turn black and needed urgent attention, Vinchenzo looked at Peters frozen foot, he turned and said to the others "we'll make camp here", the men set up the camp and started the fire for hot water and coffee, Vinchenzo called Carl to him, he told Carl to set up a look out station just inside the entrance to the cave and a perimeter around the camp with warning flares, "but only use essential personnel, allow as many of the men to rest as possible as they had a long way to go", Vinchenzo said to Carl.

"Very well sir", .

"Hopkins" Carl cried out.

"Sir" came the reply.

"Follow me!", the men left through the tunnel once more, and disappeared, after a while Carl returned and then set about laying the early warning systems using tin cans and flares.

Carl said "this would alert them to any inquisitive animals or human beings, that may want to pay them an unwelcome visit."

Ivan, asked Peter, "if he had any feeling in his foot at all, and could he feel this?"

Ivan cut across Peters foot with his knife, Peter jumped, "ouch! that hurt" he said. "Good" said Ivan, "because if it hadn't have hurt, you would be looking at losing the foot."

Peter swallowed deeply and said "lo-losing the foot, what do you mean? Now listen here I'm very fond of that foot its been everywhere with me and I'm very attached to it."

Ivan laughed, "yes I can see what you mean, now I'm going to give you a pain injection, there will be a sharp scratch then a stinging sensation, but don't worry it'll be over in a second or two."

Peter lay back as the injection began to work, the pain eased gently away, Vinchenzo returned to where Ivan and Peter where, and asked "how's Peter Ivan."

"We'll sir" Ivan replied, "he wont be able to walk properly for the next few days but he will be ok, the frost bite is superficial, although if he had been exposed for much longer he would have lost the foot."

"Good job, well done Ivan" said Vinchenzo "I'm glad he's alright, we can make a stretcher for him and we can move on."

"I'll see to right away sir" Ivan said, and went off in to the undergrowth to look for the necessary items he would need to make a stretcher.

Meanwhile Vinchenzo, called Carl over, and told him of their new plan, Carl went to fetch Hopkins and inform him of their intentions, he returned a short while later with Hopkins in tow, the men packed up camp and headed in to the bush with Peter on the stretcher, Marcella had volunteered to carry one end of the stretcher while Carl carried the other end, the men would each take two hours at carrying Peter, however Peter was not heavy and often Marcella would go four or five hours without rest.

Peter eventually woke up, he was in a tent, Marcella was sitting by his bedside reading the book he had brought with him from home, he must have read this book several times since they began their journey, Peter looked at Marcella who was by now aware that Peter had woke up, "how do you feel?" he said to Peter with a smile on his face.

"How long have I been a sleep?" Peter asked.

"Oh, about two days" Marcella replied, "now how about a nice cup of coffee eh?" asked Marcella.

"Oh, yes please" said Peter, "make that two cups if you don't mind, I've a bit of catching up to do you know."

Marcella smiled again, "yes of course" then left the tent, Marcella headed towards Ivan and told him Peter was awake now, Ivan got up and headed for the tent, "morning Peter and how's the patient today?"

Peter smiled and replied "I'm thirsty and I could eat a horse."

"Good" replied Ivan "that means your much better, how is the foot?"

"Good I think!" Peter replied "it feels quite normal."

"well lets take a look shall we?" said Ivan, he rolled back the cover and started to unwrap Peters foot, it certainly looks better said Ivan, "now lets feel it, any pain here Peter when I touch it?"

Peter squirmed and giggled "no but your tickling."

"Good" said Ivan "you can get up now, everything seems normal now."

Peter flung back the covers and went to get out of bed, he felt light headed and fell backwards, "steady Peter" said Marcella who had re-entered the tent, "you need to take things easy for the next few hours, your strength needs to return and the effects of that injection needs to ware off."

"Yes I suppose your right Marcella."

Just then Vinchenzo entered the tent, "good to have you back with us Peter, we thought we were going to have to fly you out to hospital!"

"Thank you" said Peter, "I'm glad you didn't have to send me home, especially after making it this far"

Vinchenzo smiled and said, "yes you're a though old cookie", Vinchenzo, went on to say, "we'll leave in the morning; that way your strength and balance should have been fully restored, see you at dinner", and he left.

Peter asked Marcella "what had happened over the last few days?"

Marcella started to tell Peter about the area they were in, "its beautiful he said, there are plants here that died out a long time ago, according to botanist! there are many unexplained things here", Marcella, had an excitement in his voice that Peter had not heard in a long time, it was that excitement that had first led them to go on this adventure, it was as if they had discovered a land time had forgotten.

Peter had recovered well from his ordeal and was raring to go, the next morning he was up before all the others and had stoked up the fire and the coffee pot was on, the aroma filled the camp, Peter; crouched by the fire, he was about to have his third cup of coffee when Marcella joined him, "you're up early aren't you Peter?" Marcella remarked as he smiled,

"Well you know" replied Peter "I've been asleep along time you know! and a man can only take so much rest, I need to get my limbs working, and ready for today's activities", Peter smiled back at Marcella, who was sipping his coffee, everyone was up by now and a hive of activity took place, after a while.

Vinchenzo appeared "ok men lets move!"

Everyone picked up their gear and were about to move out, when Hopkins appeared from out of now were, he went up to Carl and spoke to him, then Carl approached Ivan, and Vinchenzo, Vinchenzo looked up at Carl "are you sure he said?"

Carl replied "apparently so sir!"

Vinchenzo said to the men "ok we must move and move now!"

The men hurried themselves up and they moved off in a north easterly direction, they move quickly and silently, as if they were shadows in the night.

It wasn't long before they reached a clearing in the dense growth, Vinchenzo motioned them to halt by raising his right hand, the men crouched down were they where and waited for the next command, they didn't have to wait long before Vinchenzo once again motioned this time for them to move slowly forward and to stay down as low as possible, the men moved forward keeping low across the clearing, they reached the other side and then waited, just then out of nowhere came a small group of men, they were dressed in a style of Viking wear from long ago, suddenly Vinchenzo stood up and went over to them, the leader hugged Vinchenzo after a short while Vinchenzo motioned the men to come out, they came forward, Peter, Marcella "come here I want you to meet my old friend Kristian Tormso, he is the last of the Viking warriors we will follow him."

The men all left together and headed west into the interior, Kristian told Vinchenzo that some men had entered the kingdom shortly after they had and had set up camp near the river, Vinchenzo asked "if Kristian knew who they were?"

He said "I think they are German, other than that no, but they are heavily armed." Vinchenzo thought to himself for a moment and then said "they must be some of Von Helgar' men."

"Do you want me to take care of them?" asked Kristian

"Not for the moment" said Vinchenzo, then walking ahead of the group Vinchenzo, explained his suspicions as to Von Helgar being one of his own men, as this would explain how Von Helgar was always able to get ahead of them.

Kristian asked "if Vinchenzo knew who it was?"

Vinchenzo just looked at Kristian and said "I have a suspicion but that's all I'm going to say at this point!"

Kristian agreed, but said "I will alert my men to trust no one but you."

"Good" Vinchenzo said "as this will avert suspicion and lull him into a false sense of security."

"When will he make his move do you think?" Kristian asked!

"Well it will have to be soon, if he is to lose us as he thinks he has the only map, he'll want to get well ahead of us, tonight perhaps, but I'm not really sure" said Vinchenzo.

Kristian asked "do you want us to catch him trying to leave the camp?."

"No" Vinchenzo replied "just follow him and see which way he goes, we will then try to head him off, we can't afford to lose him and the only place we can safely deal with him is at the gateway."

Kristian replied "the Gateway? You don't mean "the Gateway?"

"Yes" Vinchenzo replied "I do! But you know the dangers that lay ahead, it's a long and dangerous road, we have travelled that road together on many occasion old friend and lost many a good man!"

Kristian replied "yes I know."

Vinchenzo said "but there is no other way!"

Kristian looked at Vinchenzo and said "as long as you have thought about it, I'm happy to accompany you all the way", then he turned and called to a man who joined them, "this is my son, Hamar, he is soul trustworthy! I give him to you to protect Peter with his life."

Vinchenzo looked at Kristian and smiled, "I should have known I could never keep a secret from you, you old goat", the men laughed and hugged.

Peter wondered what was going on, he asked Ivan "what was happening?"

Ivan replied "don't worry Peter, its just old friends reminiscent of times long past."

Peter returned to the coffee pot and the company of Marcella, while Vinchenzo and the other men carried on laughing.

Peter looked around the village it was a large settlement that had a large building in the centre, this was the large meeting house known as the long house, there were lots of people moving in and out of the village trading goods and wares, the village was near to the river, at the edge of the river was a jetty with what looked like a Viking long boat tied up at the jetty, Peter knew this because he had studied Viking history at University, he was fascinated to think, here he was in a present day Viking environment which had not changed in thousands of years, Peter thought no one would ever believe him if he told them!

Marcella appeared from what seemed out of nowhere and said "come on Peter lunch is ready", Peter, turned and headed off with Marcella towards the main meeting house and lunch.

After lunch, Peter and Marcella headed for their hut, which had been allocated to then by Hamar, Peter was still a bit groggy from his ordeal of the past few day and felt all this excitement was far too much too soon, and needed to lay down for a while, Marcella, also felt tired so they lay on the beds provided, they sank into the comfortable beds, Peter groaned with pleasure as he lay in this warm comfortable bed, he had dreamed of laying in such a bed for a long time, this was truly heaven he thought and before long he had drifted into a long comfortable sleep.

Vinchenzo and the other men checked their equipment and prepared for the next leg of their journey to the great falls, Vinchenzo and Kristian talked over the plans with Ivan, Hindrich, Carl and Hamar.

Kristian, suggested "it would take two day by boat to reach the falls, as this was the quickest way, if they went by land it would take several days and much danger", the men agreed the boats were the best idea, and prepared to move out the next day.

That night Kristian and Hamar, kept a close eye on the village, at around two in the morning, Hamar was alerted to movement in the area around the village, he crept forward in a stealth like manner until he could hear voices and make out three silhouettes, in the distance, he move forward again, he could now see the men and he lay in wait.

The men crept towards the waiting boats, they boarded the first boat so as to climb over into second and then boarded the boat which lay on the outboard side, Hamar, quietly entered the water and swam to the first boat, he clung on the side of the boat just out of sight of the intruders , he heard a voice say, "cut the boats adrift, by the time this lot realise we'll be long gone."

"Yes sir" replied one of the men, Hamar, recognised Ivan's voice, he could hear the men cutting at the ropes, he stayed motionless as the boats drifted into the main stream of the river, then when he felt it safe he climbed aboard the boat he was clinging to and steered it back to shore, by this time the other boat had disappeared around the bend of the river heading for the falls, Hamar alerted Vinchenzo and his father.

Vinchenzo asked, "Did you see who they were?"

Hamar lent forward towards Vinchenzo, and whispered, "it was Ivan, I recognised his voice and the two men that camped by the river."

Vinchenzo looked shocked, as he had always trusted Ivan, and treat him like a son, "are you absolutely sure?" he said.

Hamar replied "yes positive!"

Vinchenzo pondered the thought of Ivan being the traitor and it did begin to make sense the more he thought about it the more sense it made.

Peter leaned over towards the men to try to hear what was being said, Marcella nudge him and said "don't be so nosy Peter, if Vinchenzo wanted us to know he would have told us."

Vinchenzo turned to face the men, he began by saying "I now know why Von Helgar always seemed to be one step ahead of the game in matters concerning the Map and the pursuit of it, I have just learned that Ivan", he paused for a moment, Peter thought he was going to say

Ivan had been killed by Von Helgar, and that he had stolen a longboat and sailed for the falls, then, just then Peter became aware of Vinchenzo had started to speak again.

Vinchenzo, started to speak again, "Ivan" he repeated, "was in fact Von Helgar!"

Everyone stood a gasp for a moment, "are you sure sir" said Hindrich!

Vinchenzo replied "yes almost certainly, it was Ivan who crept out during the night and met with two of his assassins just beyond the tree line at the rivers edge, Hamar, followed them to the boats. lucky enough Hamar had the foresight to enter the water and cling on to the inside boat, while Ivan and his accomplices cut the rope setting the boats free, he was then able in the dark to steer the boat back to shore, then alert us or else we would have had a several days march ahead of us."

Ivan, Peter looked at Vinchenzo in disbelief and repeated the concern of the others "are you absolutely sure?"

Vinchenzo once again replied "yes there can be no doubt, Carl has informed me Ivan has gone along with my holdall with the other map in it!"

Peter once again asked, "Why would he need your map Vinchenzo?"

Vinchenzo replied, my map show things his map doesn't, so we need to move fast, we must reach the serpents pass before Von Helgar."

The men readied themselves to leave, Peter saw the large meeting hut and headed for it, Marcella ran after him, "Peter! Peter! Were are you going he asked?"

Peter turned and replied "for the coffee pot, I'll need all the help I can get he said."

Marcella pulled him back, "no time for that now!"

Peter felt himself dragged back he turned and looked at the coffee brewing on the stove, "but! But! I need a cup of coffee!"

Marcella said, "Later!"

Peter just looked on, as the sight and smell of all that lovely coffee faded in the distance, and before he knew it he was on the long ship and heading up river, he thought I really must teach these guys there is seldom anything more important than coffee break.

Dawn broke over the river as they entered what could only be described as a Fjord, there in the distance Peter could see what looked like whales topping the surface only they were much larger than anything he had ever seen, he looked towards the sky and he could see birds of the rarest species and even some that science thought extinct!, the waters were full of wildlife, even the fish looked prehistoric, they continued all day along the edge of the fjord until evening, when they pulled into an outlet.

Vinchenzo asked Kristian "why they had diverted from their natural course?"

Kristian told Vinchenzo "that this was a little known short cut to the falls, and if they continued till dawn they would arrive at least six hours before Von Helgar and his men, this would give them plenty of time to get a warm welcome ready for him!"

Vinchenzo said, "good, we will give him a welcome worthy of his status."

The men in the boat jumped on to the land and uncovered piles of cut logs which they spread over the ground, then ropes were thrown to them and every body got out of the boat and heaved on the ropes, even Peter helped, the boat left the water.

As they pulled, the boat rose up onto the land and over the poles, as the rear poles were exposed so they were rushed to the front of the boat and laid down once again in front of the boat, this went on for some three hours, Peter was starting to feel exhausted as was the other men, when suddenly they entered a clearing and the edge of the fjord was once again visible.

The boat lurched towards the waters edge, and on into the water once more, Peter was so relieved that was over, the men boarded once more and the long ship drifted freely down river, Peter could hear a loud roaring noise just up ahead or so he thought, Peter said to Marcella "can you hear it?"

Marcella looked at Peter and said "hear what?"

Peter replied "that noise! It sounds like thunder"

Marcella said "yes Peter it must be the great falls, we must be close now!"

Peter replied "yes we must be."

Vinchenzo stood at the brow of the long ship, they were emerging from the mouth of the estuary, the falls began to come into sight, they were so majestic in appearance, these were the biggest falls Peter had ever seen and he had visited the Victoria and the mighty Niagara falls in both Africa and Canada, but they were no bigger than this sight, Peter gasped at it size, there were birds flying around the falls and the jungle below looked dense and impassable, the water cascaded down from a seemingly endlessly high point, you could not see the top of the falls for the water mist that rose from the jungle floor.

The boat lurched against the side of the embankment and the men alighted, three men were to stay with the boat while the others went on a head, the three crew members would keep the boat out of sight so as not to alert Von Helgar and his men to their presence, the advance party would leave now, the rest of the men in a few hours just before full light.

Peter headed to the edge of the forest to collect wood for a fire, he got a fire going and put on the coffee.

Marcella asked "was it a good idea to light a fire wouldn't that alert Ivan to their presence?" Marcella kept calling Von Helgar, Ivan, this was because he was used to calling him Ivan. ,

Peter said you mean "Von Helgar?"

Marcella said "yes sorry I must stop calling him Ivan! But its difficult."

Peter replied, "I know what you mean", and put out the fire, making sure that all traces of it had been obliterated from view, Peter then opened his flask which he had filled with coffee while they were still in camp, he had remembered what one of the men had told him about putting it in his flask, yes it was cold but it still met the need he thought!

Soon, the men were up and off, they headed for the foot of the falls, it took about four hours to reach the falls, then Vinchenzo told Carl "to look for a passageway behind the wall of water", it wasn't long before he returned.

Carl went up to Vinchenzo and said "I've found the way up sir."

Vinchenzo looked at Carl and said "how far is it and how difficult?"

Carl replied, "about two hundred metres in a westerly direction, but it looks like could be difficult a climb sir, for the likes of Peter, however I'm sure he'll make it with a little help."

"Good" Vinchenzo replied, Then lets move out shall we, the soon we make the ascent the better for all concerned."

The men headed for the water fall and the wall of water that hid the way up, the climb was long and hard but nonetheless they made it, Vinchenzo thought to himself, Carl was right in his assumption, it was hard on Peter, but he did make it alright.

It was mid afternoon by now and to Peter it felt like he was on top of the world, he could see for miles there were valleys and mountains everything looked untouched the colours were vibrant, the sky bluer than he had ever seen it, the water was crystal clear, he could see golden nuggets on the bottom of a pool of water, he leant down to pick some up, as he did, he held not only gold but precious gems as well, Peter put them all back and walked on, Peter wasn't interested in this kind of stuff, he was more interested in adventure and pots of boiling hot aromatic coffee, his needs where that of a simple man.

They came to a cave entrance and set up camp for the night, they had got a head of Von Helgar and the others by a full day, and now they were ahead for the first time they would not relinquish this lead, Vinchenzo would see to that.

Peter asked Vinchenzo "if he could now get the coffee brewing?"

Vinchenzo said, "Ok but make sure you leave no evidence of it when we leave in morning!"

Peter replied, "yes Father Vinchenzo" with a skip in his voice.

Vinchenzo smiled, thinking to himself Peter will always call me Father Vinchenzo! Peter set about organising a fire and got the coffee going, Peter was aware that two of the men were sitting over on the rock near to where he was making the coffee, he overheard them laughing one said "Peter does love his coffee, and the other one said listen let me tell you Peter's my favourite! its his coffee that kept most of us awake when we were cold and wet we knew exactly were we could get a fresh pot of coffee I missed that when he was ill I'll tell you!"

Peter smiled and thought its nice to be of use and appreciated now and again, then he returned to making the coffee, in what seemed a short while the coffee was hot and the aroma filled the air, everyone headed for the pot and drank the lovely hot liquid, poor Peter thought it would all be gone before he could get a cup full, but there was plenty to go around even for Peter to have an extra cup.

Next morning the group arose early and they started out for the Serpents Pass, this would be the final leg of this part of the journey as here the showdown must begin, Von Helgar had to be stopped here or all would be lost, the men set off in small groups so as not to be caught in one large group so that if a trap were to be sprung by Von Helgar and his men he would only get a small part of the expedition and not the whole of it.

It was coming up to midday when Peter looked up, the sun was high in the heavens and the heat was almost unbearable, when Vinchenzo held up his hand and the group stopped, out of the trees came Carl.

Carl approached Vinchenzo and said "all clear up ahead sir, we've found the path that leads to the pass, shall we start ascending?"

Vinchenzo replied "very well, carry on."

Carl said "yes sir" and disappeared again, Vinchenzo motioned Peter and Marcella to move on, the men moved forward towards Vinchenzo, they came to an opening in the jungle, this was were they would wait in ambush for Von Helgar and his men, just beyond the other side of the opening was the path that led to the pass.

Peter and Marcella walked towards the path, Vinchenzo was just ahead of them with the main party which was now heading up the pathway while Hamar and three other men sat in wait for Ivan to arrive with his men, they didn't have to wait long when they heard Ivan approaching, the men waited until Ivan, and his henchmen passed by. Hamar and the others followed silently and swiftly behind, they came up behind the men killing two of them and taking Ivan prisoner, the men quickly caught up with the main group who had now reached the pass, the main group waited for Hamar to catch up with Ivan in tow, Hamar approached Vinchenzo and whispered in his ear "we have him sir!."

Vinchenzo replied "good bring him here", Hamar, returned to his waiting men and brought Ivan to the waiting group, Vinchenzo looked at Ivan, he paused and said "why?"

Ivan looked at him, and said "how long have you known it was me?"

Vinchenzo replied "not until last night for certain but then it made a lot of sense, as you were always the one to find Von Helgar' hideouts, but why sacrifice all those men, I assume you are the infamous Von Helgar?"

Ivan looked at him and said "well its of no consequence now, yes I'm he the illusive Von Helgar as you put it and as for sacrificing those men, well lets just call it collateral damage shall we", then in a flash he grabbed Hamar and pulled out a concealed knife from his sleeve, he held it to Hamar' throat, "back off" he said "or I'll kill him!"

Vinchenzo told the men to back off, "let him go we'll catch up with him sooner or later now we know his identity", the men backed off, all but Kristian who stood there, he wouldn't move away, "let my son go or so help me I'll hunt you down and kill you!"

Ivan said "now, now, you both know I can't kill him or else I'll not be able to enter the garden will I" and at that, he pushed Hamar to the ground and disappeared into trees.

Peter ran forward "are you alright Hamar ?"

"Yes thank you Peter" said Hamar picking himself up from the ground.

Vinchenzo said, "he's alright, ok lets move we've got to get to the "Gateway" before Ivan!", the men quickly moved off and into the night, it was early morning when they approached the "Gateway".

Carl who as at point came down the path and reported to Vinchenzo that all was clear, meanwhile Hamar, came up the rear, Vinchenzo asked him if Ivan was on his way?

Hamar said "yes sir he's about an hour behind us."

"Good" said Vinchenzo, "then we best move out!"

The team headed for the "Gateway" it was about two hours ahead, Peter was talking with Marcella, he said "what is the "Gateway"?"

Marcella replied, "you'll find out soon enough!"

Peter looked at Marcella and said "I know! I know! But I'd still like know what he means by the "Gateway"."

Marcella smiled, "come on Peter lets go the others are leaving."

The men started along the path, the pathway was overgrown; no one had passed this way in a long time Peter thought to himself as the undergrowth wrapped around his feet, "hurry up Peter" said Marcella "we are falling behind."

Peter looked at Marcella and said "I'm going as fast as I can its all this vegetation its slowing me down."

The men reached the entrance to the gateway, Vinchenzo, held up his hand and the team stopped, Carl stood near the entrance and Vinchenzo, asked Carl "to check the area out for insurgence that may try to ambush the team", Carl headed off in a easterly direction, mean while Vinchenzo told Peter and the other men to prepare camp, Peter headed for the trees to collect fire wood, he was merrily collecting wood! When from out of nowhere Peter, felt a hand move over his mouth, he struggled but to no avail, who ever had grabbed him was strong, Peter felt a sharp pain in his leg and then he felt himself drift into a dreamy sleep.

Some time had passed when Vinchenzo, asked Marcella, "were is Peter?"

Marcella said "I thought he was with you!"

Vinchenzo replied "no, I thought I seen him head for the edge of the jungle."

Vinchenzo, alerted the men and they began to search the edge of the jungle, Hamar found Peters St Christopher on the ground near a clump of trees where the undergrowth was flattened, he called over Vinchenzo and Marcella, "looks like a struggle took place over here sir and I've found this."

Marcella took hold of the St Christopher saying, "this belongs to Peter", with a lump in his throat.

Hamar said, "it looks like Ivan's got Peter!"

"Yes" replied Vinchenzo, Vinchenzo then said in a reassuring voice "don't worry Marcella Von Helgar won't hurt him, he needs him as much as we do."

Marcella asked Vinchenzo "what do you mean? he needs Peter as much as we do"

Vinchenzo began to explain to Marcella, "Peter is the only one amongst us who can enter the serpents lair, only a human can enter and release the mechanism to allow us to pass through."

"Us?" Marcella said, "What do you mean us?"

Vinchenzo explained to Marcella "how he was now a guardian as well he was immortal and no longer mortal, he had died in the castle and was favoured by God to help protect the scroll, you must have know something special had happened to you when you woke from that deep sleep?"

Marcella replied "well yes I did feel different even in the shoot outs I swore I saw a bullet hit me but it seemed to go straight through, but then I thought I was imagine things."

Vinchenzo replied "no you weren't imagining it at all Marcella!"

Marcella sat down trying to take all this in, "you mean I'm really dead?"

Vinchenzo said "don't look at it as your dead, but more as you are spirit therefore, not of this world, yet in it, you are immortally alive!"

Hamar said to Marcella "don't worry this is a normal reaction, I felt the same when I found out."

Marcella turned to Hamar and said "you mean you are also immortal!"

Hamar said "yes, me too"

Marcella then said "but your father seemed concerned over the fact that Von Helgar was going to kill you?"

Hamar replied "yes I know, but that you know how over protective parents get, and besides it was to make things seem normal to Ivan therefore, not alerting him to my real status!"

Marcella went on to say "you mean he doesn't know?"

Hamar replied "no he doesn't know as he is from the pit not the heavens; he is stuck on this planet with no means of escape because of his deceit, he is a liar and an uncompromising villain that's why he is always after the treasures of God, he keeps us busy!"

Marcella asked Vinchenzo, "How long have you know he was a villain?"

Vinchenzo replied "oh only since last night, however, his father now he's been trouble since time on earth began, he's been known as Beelzebub, Damian, and other such names, and now I suppose Ivan is part of that! Throughout the centuries he loves to use others to achieve his wicked ways and then he kills them usually making it look like suicide."

Marcella marvelled, then asked "how old is he for goodness sake?"

Hamar replied "oh, much older than Vinchenzo and my Father, no one, except our boss really knows how old Ivan or his father is."

Marcella looked at Hamar and Vinchenzo in disbelief, "am I now like him unable to die?"

Vinchenzo replied "oh no, you will die many times over but there will be no pain of death or sorrow, you will just die and rise a new, unlike Ivan who will die many times but will feel the full pain of death every time."

Marcella swallowed deeply, "now come on Marcella" said Hamar "your one of us now and the secrets of the world are yours to command."

Marcella rose from the rock he was sitting on and the men headed towards the main pack with Vinchenzo, who was now heading for the serpents lair, "come on men lets go we've a lot to do! before we can retrieve Peter because he is the only key, and we must arrive on time."

Peter eyes opened slowly, "hello Peter" a voice said, "how do you feel?"

Peter looked towards a figure standing over him, his focus was blurred then slowly returned, it was Ivan the terrible he thought, then he said "why should that concern you 'traitor' and why am I here? Come to think of it where is here?"

Ivan smiled "now, now, Peter you'll soon see" and walked off.

Peter looked around he was in some sort of cave and there were two, what looked like natives watching over him, the cave smelt of sulphur, and mould, Peter sat up his head was throbbing from the injected liquid, he tried to get up but was unable to; his legs felt like lead, he shuffled to the edge of the bed and began to push up on the rail at the foot of the bed, but he fell again, he lay back down and rested.

A short while later, Ivan returned and said to Peter "you'll feel the benefit of this injection it will help with the head and you'll feel well again in an hour or two", he took Peter's arm and placed an needle into it, Peter felt the warm liquid enter his system and then drifted off again.

Vinchenzo and the others entered the cave entrance to the serpents lair, once inside the men headed down the tunnel, it was dark and damp, yet was warm at the same time the type of place that you would expect a snake to live.

Marcella followed the others, deeper and deeper they went into the cave, every so often Hindrich, would light another torch made from a type of hair.

These lined the passage way every so often, then the men came to a large cavern, inside which was a building carved out of the rock, on the front of which looked like a giant snake similar to the one in Marcella and Peter had encountered in the Amazon some weeks ago.

Marcella marvelled at the gigantic structure which towered over them. Vinchenzo again held up his hand and said "we'll camp here tonight and enter the temple in the morning."

Everyone unhooked their packs and began to set up camp, Marcella was still trying to come to terms with his new situation, it had come as quiet a shock to realise, that one was no longer mortal but was now immortal, that he totally forgot about Peter for a moment, then suddenly as he realised that Peter was not preparing the coffee, he went over to where Vinchenzo was, "are you alright Marcella?" asked Vinchenzo.

"Yes I seem to be coming to terms with my situation now, but its Peter I'm more worried about at the moment."

Vinchenzo replied "oh I shouldn't be overly concerned if I were you he'll be here shortly as this is the only way to the gateway, he must first pass the test of time before anyone can enter and pass to the "Gateway"."

Marcella asked "what are these test?"

Vinchenzo, replied "the only person allowed to take the test, must be male and without blemish, we immortals cannot take the test as it can only be the Son of Adam anyone else including us would only release the serpent and although it could not harm us it could destroy the world if prematurely released!"

Marcella thought for a moment, then said "that's why it must be Peter he is the only one who is mortal?"

Vinchenzo replied, "that's right! and that's why we must allow Ivan to use Peter to open the way to the "Gateway"."

Marcella once again thought deeply about the situation, then said "but if Ivan gets Peter through the tests won't we have lost?"

Vinchenzo looked at Marcella, and said, "not really! but Ivan thinks like you and that's what we want him to think, you see what he doesn't know is as soon as Peter opens the way, Ivan will immediately follow, however one of the safety measures built in to the passage is that only the pure may enter. As soon as Ivan enters the way he will be cast in to the pit with his master the serpent! there to remain forever more, until his release by our Master, when he returns to judge him and the beast, for there crimes against God and humanity."

Marcella felt much better now knowing Peter was about to be saved, by now the camp was up and ready; the coffee was brewing, Marcella was thinking of poor Peter once more he looked towards the far end of this huge expanse of cave to what looked like an entrance to a temple of some sort, he thought once more to himself I do hope Peter can fulfil these "Test of Time" whatever they were, Marcella became aware that Vinchenzo had begun to say something and thought he had better listen closely. Vinchenzo by saying "that they should all get some sleep, they would make an early start the next day", Vinchenzo, then turned to Carl and said "post centuries to keep a close watch for Ivan and his cronies, so as they would not be surprised by any of Ivan's tricks."

Carl replied, should I prepare a few surprises further inside the tunnel as well sir." Vinchenzo replied, "whatever you think necessary"

Carl said "Very well sir", and left with two other men.

Vinchenzo, suggested they should sleep light and be ready to move at a moments notice, all of the men agreed and they settled down for the night.

CHAPTER 8
The Gateway

In the morning Vinchenzo woke Marcella, "quickly, we must move Ivan is almost on top of us with Peter, they must not see us or know we are here or else all is lost ."

Marcella quickly got up and helped wipe out all evidence of them being there ahead of Ivan, he then grabbing his gear ran to where the others were, they crouched behind one corner of the Temple, Vinchenzo could see the flickering lights coming up the passage way, they were close now.

Vinchenzo held up his hand in a motion to alert them to stay very still and quiet as any sound or unnecessary motion could give them away, just then Ivan and two natives appeared from the tunnel, he motioned them to check out the area, the men circled the area and then gave the all clear, Peter emerged with two other men, with Ivan following close behind, Ivan, walked towards the entrance to the Temple, he beckoned the men forward.

Ivan said, "now Peter I want you to come with me, the rest of you stay here and keep guard, stay alert mind! or you'll wish you'd never met me!."

Vinchenzo and the team waited for Ivan to disappear into the temple then Vinchenzo motioned to Carl, to take out the guards, he moved quietly and swiftly, with one movement, he and the two men with him slit the throats of the guards, they slumped to the ground then Vinchenzo, and the others came from behind the temple wall and headed for were Carl was.

Vinchenzo looked at Carl and said "well done Carl."

Carl replied "thank you sir."

Vinchenzo, then said to three of the men "take up position near to the entrance of the temple but to stay out of sight just in-case Ivan, had more men on their way." the men acknowledged Vinchenzo, then took up their positions ready to take care of any insurgence that may try to impede their progress.

Meanwhile, Vinchenzo, motioned the other men to follow him into the temple, the men walked through the entrance of the temple and into the entrance hall, it was enormous inside, the roof domed into a large pinnacle, the walls were inlaid with gold and precious gems, these reflected the light, it acted as a large chandelier, at the end of the main hall there was a door way like a huge pearl! The light reflected from it causing a prism of light to the centre of the floor as if guiding the weary traveller on into the doorway.

The men proceeded towards the entrance of the door, there was a strong odour that left one feeling like, something or someone had died and was decaying, Vinchenzo led the way through the doorway and on down a long dark passageway, the only light came from the torches that Carl had lit as he led them down the passage, the passageway was hewn out of the rock as if someone or something had bored its way through, the men continued down the passageway until they came to a bend in the passage.

Vinchenzo motioned the men to stop, "put out the torches" he said "we are close to the main chamber and that's where Ivan and Peter will be."

The men dowsed the torches and moved forward slowly through the dark winding passage way, Marcella fumbled his way along the passage, all he could think of was Peter at the mercy of Ivan or Von Helgar or whoever he was, Marcella just wanted Peter safe, he had missed Peter these last few days, as Peter, always loved to brew up the coffee, the aroma of that coffee had been sorely missed not because Marcella loved coffee that much, but just because it meant he missed Peter.

The men by now could see a faint light up a head of them, Vinchenzo once again stopped the men, ok Vinchenzo said "we are very close now,

Carl take two men and secure the tunnel, make sure no one can follow, just in-case we have unexpected company!"

Carl acknowledged by saying "very well sir should I seal the passage?"

Vinchenzo replied "no just secure it", Carl, and two of his men stayed back while Vinchenzo and the others proceeded.

Back outside the temple entrance, Hamar, and his colleagues heard voices coming from the tunnel leading to the entrance to the temple, Hamar, lay in wait to see who was about to appear, several the men emerged from the tunnel, "Hamar said to his men "Vinchenzo was right it was Von Helgar' men he must have got a message out some how and it looks like they were on their way to reinforce him", Hamar, said to the men "wait for my signal before you opened fire", the men nodded to show they acknowledged and understood his order.

Suddenly, several of Von Helgar' men appeared from the tunnel, they moved forward as if totally unaware of any resistance.

Suddenly Hamar yelled, "open fire" and a number of Von Helgar' men fell to the ground in what looked like a heap, the others retreated back into the cave, Hamar was unsure how many men were left but he estimated around three or four, Hamar waited and then told the men to advance, shots rang out from inside the tunnel, the men threw themselves to the ground and returned fire, then got up quickly and advanced once again, more shots rattled out, the men once again threw themselves to the ground and returned fire, the sound of men being hit was heard from within the tunnel, and the men once again quickly stood up and advanced, once inside the tunnel Hamar found four bodies, the incursion had been successfully eliminated.

Hamar and the men checked for evidence of other insurgents but none was found, they had caught them totally by surprise, just then Carl appeared from inside the temple, he had heard the ruckus, while searching the tunnel for a good place to ambush any infiltrators, "Hamar is everything ok?"

Hamar appeared from within the other tunnel, "yes thanks Carl we caught them by surprise!"

Carl replied "good I'm glad you're ok, now lets go and join the others, I've rigged up an early warning system just inside the doorway to the throne room, we'll keep watch from there Just in case we have anymore unwelcome guest."

Hamar nodded and the men entered the temple, once inside they entered the passage that led to the inner chamber and throne room.

Vinchenzo and the others were now nearing the entrance to the inner chamber, they stayed in the shadows, just out of sight of Ivan and the others. Ivan was looking at the entrance that would lead to the great "Gateway" but knew only Peter could clear the way for him to pass, Peter was being held by two burly looking natives, over the entrance of the passage was carved a gigantic serpent, it looked almost alive, Marcella, remarked to Vinchenzo "just how life like this serpent was."

Vinchenzo turned, and looking at Marcella he replied "it is real! It is in a deep sleep and can only be wakened by Peter making a mistake or by some one unworthily trying to open the way to the "Great Gate"."

Marcella notice what looked like skeletons marring the way to the throne beyond which lay the path to the "Great Gate", he asked Vinchenzo "who are they do you think?"

Vinchenzo replied, "oh, they are a mixture of sacrificial offerings to the great serpent and unworthy men who got greedy and tried to retrieve the riches beyond the "Great Gate" over the centuries, their greed, besotted them into believing they were the chosen ones."

Marcella replied "chosen ones! chosen ones! What do you mean chosen ones?"

Vinchenzo started to explain to Marcella "that only those chosen by God and pure in motive could ever proceed further than the throne and once through! Open the passage to angels and guardians!"

Marcella asked, "so how do we know that Peter is a chosen one?"

Vinchenzo replied "we don't not until he tries!"

Marcella stood mouth open wide and blurted out "so that means he could perish! said Marcella?"

Vinchenzo replied "yes in theory that's true."

Marcella once again was aghast "yes theoretically! Yes theoretically!" replied Marcella in a voice that was beginning to panic, "theoretically yes! Well that's a bit hit and miss he said, what if poor Peter perishes in the act of trying to complete the tasks set for him?"

Vinchenzo looked at Marcella, "we don't think like that he said, for if he fails we all fail and the guardians are no more!".

Back in the cave Ivan, motioned his men to bring Peter forward, Peter stood by Ivan and Ivan began to explain what Peter must do, then Peter asked "and if I refuse!"

Ivan looked at Peter and smiled, "don't even go there" said Ivan, "for if we try to leave now the serpent will be aroused and have us for lunch!"

Peter said "what do you mean?"

Ivan began to explain, "you see Peter the moment we entered the throne room a series of acts went into motion, these acts activated certain elements which prevent us leaving, go ahead and try if you don't believe me" he said.

Peter said "what you mean I can go! if I want?"

Ivan replied "you can try! but remember this, the moment you try to leave this cavern the serpent will wake and we are all dead!"

Peter looked into Ivan's eyes, he was deadly serious, Peter could also see the fear in the native's eyes, "ok! ok! what do I have to do?"

Ivan said to Peter "you're the only one who can answer that!"

Peter wondered what he meant by that, and he turned to look at Ivan, and asked him "what he meant?"

Ivan replied "search your heart and trust your feelings Peter", Peter walked towards the throne, as he did he remember his grandmothers words, when you are in danger just recite the twenty third psalm, so he began reciting to himself the twenty third psalm,

> *"The Lord is my shepherd I shall not be in want.*
> *He makes me lie down in green pastures, he leads*
> *me beside quiet waters, he restores my soul.*
> *He guides me in paths of righteousness for his name's sake.*
> *Even though I walk through the valley of the shadow*
> *of death, I will fear no evil for you are with me."*

Peter continued toward the throne and the entrance to the cave that would eventually lead him to the "Great Gateway" that lay beyond the throne room of the serpent, Peter saw a plaque above the throne, which said

"Abandon All Hope Ye Who Dare To Pass This Way! As Only The Pure In Heart May Do So, As God Himself Shall Be Your Judge."

Peter looked up and nervously and swallow, he wanted to turn back but something or someone was leading him to go on, as he continued through to the entrance, he noticed several oddly dressed skeletons, they looked like they were from a long lost civilisation, then he remembered where he had seen such a dress code it was from the early Hittite civilisations, he also notice some skeletons were dressed in Roman uniforms, as he kicked through the bones he noticed yet more strangely dressed skeletons even that of a German S/S uniform, he thought to himself these must be the missing expeditions from ancient and modern times, but they never made it any further, Peter looked towards the entrance of the cave, there in one corner near the entrance was another plaque this time it said "Stand And Be Judged At Your Own Peril."

Peter stood for awhile wondering what this mean, he felt an urge to draw near to the plaque, he waited, then stepped forward on to the spot, after a moment a ray of light engulfed him the light was so bright that the others had to look away, for the light was too bright for the human eyes, Peter could see Ivan and the others knelt and turned away from where he was, then Peter was suddenly aware that he could see Vinchenzo and the others deep in the cave, he called out "Vinchenzo, Marcella I'm here" Marcella obviously could not hear him, but Vinchenzo could, he looked at Peter and said "fear not Peter for the Lord is with you", then the light stopped, Peter thought he was dreaming but also felt a new confidence, he walked forward into the cave, he was out of sight of the others now and as he walked it seemed his path was light by some mysterious light, then he remembered in the psalms that he had been taught to remember it said, in psalm 119:.

"The word is a lamp onto your feet and a light unto my path."

Peter felt in his inside coat pocket and pulled out his little travelling Bible, which his grandmother always insisted he carried, normally it would have been in his rucksack, but they had been in such a rush the other day, that he had slipped it into his inside pocket, Peter often read his Bible at night before he went to bed, but for some reason he had got it out the other day while resting against the rock at the foot of the pass, he was at this point grateful he had, Peter opened the Bible, it opened at the book of Isaiah, chapter 41: he looked down at the verse, it was verse 10 it said,

"So do not fear, for I am with you; do not be
dismayed, for I am your God."

Peter felt strangely close to God for some reason closer than he had ever felt before, he thought am I really a chosen one, or is it all about to go sour and I end up snake bait? Peter stopped, hold on a moment he though, God has never let me down so come what may I'll carry on, in faith I'll walk, then he started up the path singing,

"My Jesus my saviour, Lord there is none like you.
All of my days I want to praise the wonders of your Love"

Peter came to a large cavern, there he stopped, looked around just in-case of unexpected surprises, then he noticed in the middle of the cavern stood a man dressed all in white, he beckoned Peter to come to him as Peter approached he could see a fire and on it a pot, his eyes lit up, it was a coffee pot and the aroma was almost heavenly, "come a long Peter" the old man said.

Peter hesitated for a moment, "how do you know my name?" he said rather wearily. "oh I know a lot about you Peter, I've been watching you since before you were born, when you were still in your mothers womb."

Peter looked puzzled and a bit afraid, "don't be afraid Peter", said the man, he had a warm looking face and was totally dressed in white, yet a voice of authority as if a great king.

Peter headed for the coffee pot and poured himself a cup, then began to tell the man of the plight he was in, the man looked at Peter and said "do not worry about what will happen or where you will go from here, just trust in me."

Peter felt reassured somehow by his words, he felt like he had known him all of his life somehow it was the strangest feeling, Peter supped the coffee and was about to say I must go on now, but stopped! Somehow, he new that there was no need to say anything.

Peter, got up from the fireside, as he did, he turned to thank the man and say goodbye but the man had gone he had disappeared, vanished in a flash, Peter could not see him anywhere, then he remembered the story of Jesus and the start of his ministry and how he had been tempted by the devil forty days and forty nights and at the end of which angels came to minister to him, to give him strength for what lay ahead.

Peter walked on into another tunnel, there he could see another great light he headed for it, it led to another chamber, there another old man dressed in white sat waiting for him, this time there was a plate of the most wonderful fruits, "take eat" said the man and sat on a rock, "come sit Peter", he said.

Peter was astonished that this man too knew his name, "tell me Peter why are you here?"

Peter explained "that unless he reached the end of his journey he and his friends would die, but if he could reach the end and successfully complete the mission his friends would live."

The man asked "and what about you Peter do you want to live?"

"Of course I do" replied Peter "but if it means my life or my friend's lives then I will gladly give mine!"

The old man asked "do you really mean that Peter?"

Peter replied "yes with all of my heart, I love Vinchenzo, Marcella, Hindrich and all of the other guys, they have all laid their lives down for me and I will gladly give mine for them!"

In the cave Vinchenzo waited to see what would happen, Ivan was waiting impatiently for Peter to return, when a great light filled the cave and the tunnel, it was so bright no one could look into it except Vinchenzo, who by now had changed into a cloak of white raiment, the light faded and the men suddenly found themselves in the chamber with Peter, the man had vanished just like the other fellow, Peter suddenly looked around and saw Vinchenzo and the others, "where did you come from?" he gasped, "and were is Ivan?"

"Here he is" said Marcella, peeping around the corner of everyone else, Marcella! cried Peter and ran up and hugged him so hard poor Marcella had to ask Peter to let him go so he could breath, the men danced around in a circle, they were so pleased to see each other.

Vinchenzo came over "well done Peter."

Peter stopped and looked at Vinchenzo, "well done! for what?" he said, then replied again "I've done nothing, its you guys that deserve the praise!"

Vinchenzo smiled and looked at Marcella, and said "see I told you only Peter could have done what was needed to be done."

Marcella smiled and said "yes I realise that now!"

Peter exclaimed, "but where is Ivan?"

Marcella replied again, "here he is look" pointing to the ground.

Peter looked down at the ground and there in the dust of the cave was a large snake.

Vinchenzo said to Peter "don't worry about Von Helgar he has his reward!" And at that the ground swallowed up the snake.

"where has it gone?" asked Peter with a look of astonishment on his face.

Vinchenzo said "look closely Peter and you'll see."

Peter looked hard at the ground suddenly it opened up to reveal a deep dark pit, in it he could see a dragon type creature, and a smaller one with it they were chained to the wall of the pit, Peter looked at Vinchenzo and asked what this meant, then he turned back to look at the scene and said "I know! I know!, be patient and you will eventually tell me."

The men all laughed and Vinchenzo said to Peter "you're catching on well now!"

Peter asked Vinchenzo "what they were to do now?"

Vinchenzo replied "we must continue on with our journey for it is not completed yet, we must reach the underground river then make our accent to the surface once more, it will take a few days yet and Kristian and the others need to return home."

"Home!" Peter said "now that sound good to me."

Again the men laughed "yes you're right Peter home sounds good."

Peter said "but what about the map?"

Vinchenzo replied "oh don't you worry about the map, its in a safe place now, and where it rightfully belongs until next time!"

At that the men began to head for the tunnel which lay ahead of them, Peter asked "can't we just go back the way we came?"

"No! said Vinchenzo "that way is sealed now, only those still searching can enter that way, for those who have sort and found there is only one way out and that's ahead of us."

Peter said "but what a bout Carl and the others?"

"Oh they'll meet us back at the settlement in a week or so", said Vinchenzo.

Peter felt relieved the ordeal was all over, and the men left, Peter thought to himself who were those men? Were they really ministering angels, or were they one in the same person? he looked around at all the other men and thought oh well it doesn't really matter we are all safe now and I'm just happy to be back in the company of all my friends.

The men stopped after a couple of hours, "we'll make camp here" said Vinchenzo, Peter straight away headed to look for firewood to make a fire, there was plenty laying about so he quickly gathered up the pieces of wood and laid them in a pile, he took some paper and what looked like dry moss and lit the fire, he then headed for Marcella' rucksack, because he knew that's where the coffee was.

Peter, took a coffee pot, he then looked around for a water supply, he found a pool of clear water near the cave wall, he filled the pot and headed back for the fire, the water was soon boiling and once again Peter, filled the air with the aroma of freshly made coffee, Marcella could smell the aroma of fresh brewed coffee as could all the others, he took in a deep breath through his nostrils, he thought to himself its good to have Peter back, he had missed that wonderful aroma which he now associated with Peter, as did all the men!

Vinchenzo, walked over to Peter and knelt down beside him, and whispered "its good to have you back with us, but can we all share the coffee?"

Peter looked at Vinchenzo and said "nothing would give me more pleasure than have you all share this long awaited and well deserved mug of coffee", the men cheered and laughed then everyone joined in a welcome d cup of coffee.

They rested for several hours before continuing their journey, they had been going sometime when Vinchenzo held up his hand and asked for silence, the men stayed perfectly still and silent, "Peter come here and you also Marcella", the men approached Vinchenzo listen he said "can you hear it?"

"Hear what?" said Marcella.

"Wait a minute" said Peter, "yes I can, it sounds like water gushing along."

Vinchenzo smiled once again and said "yes Peter, it's the river, we are close now, we'll be ascending in the next few hours", he then turned to the other men and said "right prepare for the ascent!" The men prepared themselves and headed towards the sound of the water, it wasn't long before they reached the river, then started the ascent, it took some two hours to reach the surface, the men emerged onto a sight which took away the breath of all who cast their eyes over it, it was indescribable beauty, Peter had never seen anything like it before, from where they stood Peter could see for miles.

There was a forest floor, with all kinds of animals wondering aimlessly about, he could see a massive waterfall that cascaded down to the forest floor, the rising mist was the water falling and in the midst of all this a clearing with what looked like a "Great Gateway", this must have been what all the fuss was about thought Peter.

The men continued down the path on to the forest floor, they headed towards the "Great Gateway" that loomed high above the forest, as they approached the gate, Peter noticed that odd combinations of animals congregated together, lion, goats and sheep were all living in harmony with one another, crocodiles, deer, and water buffalo all grazed near the rivers edge, he thought this rather odd as normally these animals would avoid each other like the plague.

Peter then looked up at the "Great Gate", it was huge as big as two articulated lorries standing one on top of the other on their heads, it was inset with precious jewels and the outside looked like a huge pearl just like the one he had seen before, it was cover in some sort of vine and in the centre there was what looked like a swirling sword of fire.

"This is as far as we can go", said Vinchenzo "we must turn and go around, we must head for the falls."

Peter asked Vinchenzo "why they could go no further?"

Vinchenzo replied "no man, nor angel may pass this point ever again, the only one to enter here must be spotlessly pure or he'll die and be lost forever!" explained Vinchenzo, "that's why it is so important for us to retrieve the map every time!

many have died trying to steal the map for their own gain and greedy ambition but none will ever succeed for if they did then all would be lost to men."

Peter continued, "you mean to say no one can enter in through this Great Gate?"

Vinchenzo replied "that's right" Peter.

Peter continued, but how can anyone enter through the "Gate" then in to the "Garden"?"

"Oh there is another gate in which one can enter through", replied Vinchenzo, "but not by this one!"

"So where is the other gate?" Peter asked.

"Search your heart Peter you know the way, its truth and light to all who seek it!"

Peter paused for a moment and thought how his gran, used to say the same thing to him, theses words were familiar to him.

Then Peter asked "where are we then? is this truly Eden?"

"Yes if you want it to be Peter", replied Vinchenzo, then men headed east out of Eden, towards the rising sun and home, hopefully, their mission accomplished.

Peter was reminiscent over the time he had spent following the trail of the map, many trials and dangers had been overcome, but more than this Peter had come to appreciate the value of life and good friends.

He had realised life was fragile and that it could be over in just a few moments, never would he take life for granted again, nor that of the company of those friends close to his heart, he now appreciated the gift of life and its fragility, he realised how lonely life could be and that of the importance of sharing in life's walk with others. loneliness is a choice that we ourselves make, and that we need not be alone if we don't want to be thought Peter.

Marcella asked Peter what he was thinking so deeply about, Peter looked at Marcella and said, "oh, just how lucky I am to have such good friends."

Marcella put his arm around Peter and said "yes I know what you mean", the men continued on there journey reminiscent of the past months, and appreciating the fact that they had survived the ordeal, before long the men stopped at the edge of a great river, "come on" said Vinchenzo "we'll make camp here tonight then in the morning we'll follow the river to the great falls and home", everyone took off their rucksacks and began to prepare camp, Peter was off as usual collecting wood for the fire and the inevitable coffee making ceremony, while Marcella, found a place to put up the tent and get the sleeping accommodation ready, Vinchenzo asked Hindrich, to look for anything that was edible.

Hindrich, set off into the glade, it was about an hour later he returned with two enormous birds, Peter looked up as Hindrich was passing, he said glibly, "we will eat well tonight with that lot, expecting guest are we!"

Hindrich smiled at Peter, "no but as your so impressed then you and Marcella won't mind cleaning the birds, he then dropped them at Peter's feet."

Marcella nudged Peter and whispered "thank you very much!"

Peter and Marcella began to laugh, Peter replied "yes one day I'll learn to keep my big mouth shut."

Hindrich smiled "yes, one day Peter, one day!"

Peter and Marcella, started to clean the wild foul Hindrich had brought them, it wasn't long before the birds were roasting quite happily on a spit that Kristian had rigged up for them, that night the whole camp ate heartily.

Next morning the men arose early and prepared to move out when Peter noticed a strange looking bird like animal, "what's that?" Peter asked

Vinchenzo replied, "oh that, that, Peter is a dodo bird".

"A dodo bird?" exclaimed Peter, "but aren't they supposed to be extinct?"

Vinchenzo replied, "only to men Peter, only to men! not to this hidden land, here they are only allowed to kill for food not sport or greed." Peter paused for a moment and thought I wished that is how the world could live, then carried on with his conversation with Vinchenzo, Peter eventually began to ask Vinchenzo what had really happened to Ivan, and why he had done what he had done, Vinchenzo began to explain to Peter as much as he dare, Peter he said "Ivan was not whom he seemed to be, we were all fooled by him, I met Ivan a long time ago, just like you he had unavoidably joined us, in those days life was far more primitive than now, he had found a certain map and was trying to stop some unsavoury people acquiring its contents, he began like you and Marcella, but unlike you and Marcella he got greedy, the draw of the treasure overcome him, it was a century or so later that Von Helgar appeared."

Peter suddenly butted in, "a century or so! how old was he for goodness sake?"

Vinchenzo looked at Peter and said, "Peter you must stop interrupting if you want to know the truth."

Peter apologised and Vinchenzo carried on, "we had become very close over the time we spent together", Vinchenzo. used the word time so as to avert Peter interrupting him again with "how old!"

Peter was astounded at what he was hearing. He kept wanting to interrupt but thought better of it in the light of what Vinchenzo had just said a few moments ago, Peter continued to listen in awe of what he was being told, the men spoke for hours, Vinchenzo said "Ivan had gone from good to evil through his desire for riches! the riches of the "Garden"."

Peter could now no-longer hold back the words that had welled up inside of him, he suddenly blurted out "but we saw riches enough, on the way to "Great Gateway" enough to satisfy any man, why couldn't he just have settled for that?"

Vinchenzo replied "yes your right Peter, but that is because you're not selfish, you would have been satisfied with that, however, Ivan or Von Helgar as we found out wanted what he could never have, that which is forbidden, he could never be satisfied with less so he sold his soul to his master, that of greed, "Mammon" is his old name and the Devil his master."

Vinchenzo went on to say "when you looked into the pit, tell me what did you see?"

Peter began to explain what he thought he saw, "I saw a great beast in chains and what looked like his spawn, a baby beast also in chains."

"Good" said Vinchenzo "you saw well, the bigger of the two beast was the father of all lies and the smaller was his apprentice!"

Peter looked astonished he said "you mean that Ivan was the apprentice?"

Vinchenzo said "well that's for you to workout in your own mind!"

Peter asked Vinchenzo "will Ivan, Von Helgar whatever you want to call him remain in the pit forever?"

Vinchenzo replied "no! unfortunately he won't, some day he will be released by mans greed once again or for the final judgement day and then judged by he who is worthy, the Lord of Lords will one day seal his fate."

At that the men reached the "Great Falls" and the gateway back into reality.

As they approached the entrance to the pathway that would lead them once more down the falls and out of the land they had entered some weeks prior they could see Hamar and Carl with the other men waiting for them.

Vinchenzo and Kristian, welcomed the men and asked if all went well, Hamar and Carl explained all that had happened and how some of Von Helgar' and said "the men had tried to get in to the temple, and that they had ambushed them leaving no prisoners."

Vinchenzo congratulate the men on a job well done, Vinchenzo, Carl, Marcella, Peter and the others returned through the mountain and the long road home, the men began the decent to the canopy floor below, at the bottom of the fall, they headed for the river where they last left the Long-ship and the awaiting men.

Kristian took out a small horn and blew it, it sounded like a great "elk" suddenly the Long-ship appeared from nowhere and the men boarded it, heading once again to the great settlement, they reached the jetty where they would be landing, and alighted the Long-ship.

Everybody, in the settlement ran to greet the conquering heroes, or that's what it seemed like to Peter, they cheered and a great feast took place that night, Peter nor Marcella had ever attended a Viking feast before, they had read much about them, but to experience it first hand was something else Peter thought to himself.

The ale flowed very feely and the banqueting table never seemed to empty, the quicker Peter seemed to eat, the more the empty plates were replenished by even more food.

Peter loved this; it was like no other party he had been to. Peter spotted what looked like an enormous coffee pot in the middle of the room, ha! he thought to himself I think I'm in heaven and ran over to the pot of steaming coffee, he looked around for a cup or mug of some kind, but all he could find was a beer horn so he emptied it out and filled it with coffee.

Meanwhile, Hamar had spotted Peter and went over to see what he was up to! as he approached Peter, he notice the coffee pot and the look of pure satisfaction on Peters face, Hamar laughed with a loud voice, "I see your happy Peter. and slapped Peter on the back, Peter was just about to swallow and savour the coffee, he shot forward and spilt the coffee all over the place, Hamar grabbed Peter just in time, "sorry Peter" he said still laughing, Peter wallowed back towards Hamar, Hamar refilled his cup and the men laughed heartily once more, Peter, "you know one day that stuff will kill you."

Peter looked at Hamar and said "I know, but until that day comes I'll enjoy every cup."

Hamar tapped Peter once more on his back, this time more gently, and said "you're alright in my book Peter, if you ever need me then just call."

Peter smiled and said "thank you, I very much like you too!"

The next morning Peter got up early and stoked up the embers of the fire and began too brew up the coffee, the aroma wafted through the camp and woke the others, it was about midday when Vinchenzo and the men prepared to leave, Kristian, Hamar and the rest of the settlement came to say farewell to the team, hugs where exchange by all and the men left.

Vinchenzo led the team back towards the ice cave, the men picked up their sealskin overcoats and boots then they dressed for the journey back to the Eskimo village that they had first started their journey from, the sledges and dogs were being looked after by the two men from the Inuit village, they had waited with the dogs on Vinchenzo' orders, just in-case anything went wrong and they would have to make a quick return to the village, the men stood up when they heard the men coming, they had their weapons at the ready just in-case they were uninvited guest.

When the men caught sight of Vinchenzo and the other men coming down the long ice passageway of the cave, they ran over to them in-case they needed help, the men headed for the sledges, and the epic journey across the ice began, it was about a day and a half's journey when they came but it would take two full days back as they weren't in such a hurry now.

They arrived back at the village and the people were once again around the edge of the settlement in order to welcome back those who were returning, Peter watched as they entered the village once more, he thought to himself, did they disperse after we left or have they not moved, as when he looked at where they were, it was as if they hadn't ever moved, as if they were still in the same positions as when they first left. Peter smiled to himself, saying don't be silly they must have moved, he was just allowing his imagination run away with him, and he thought that was not usually him.

The sledges pulled up near the big hut where they had planned their next move, they got out of the sledges, once inside the hut, Carls, adopted parents were there inside the hut.

Maria and Lopez, were handing out cups of hot coffee, Maria saw Carl, Marcella, and Peter standing in the doorway, she went over to the men carrying three hot cups of coffee on a wooden tray, she approached the men holding the tray out in front of her, the men took a cup each, then she calmly put the tray down and hugged all three men, she was obviously pleased to see them thought Peter, then he continued to drink this wonderful cup of coffee.

Just then a man walked in and in his hand was what looked like Peters favourite cup, he walked over to Peter and said "this is yours I believe?"

"Yes" Peter said, thanking the man, Peter could hardly contain his joy at retrieving his old faithful friend once more, he thought he had seen the end of the mug, he asked the man where he had got the mug, the man replied "I was out on a seal hunt and found a dead seal at the foot of the mountain, and when I looked it had your cup in its head."

Peter cringed as the man explained quite vividly how he had had to use a knife to free his cup, then suddenly everyone burst into laughter, Peter looked around, "oh, very funny" he said, "very funny!" Peter then began to laugh himself when he thought of the ridiculousness of the situation, the men ate a hearty meal that night and celebrate once more their victory over the greed of man.

Peter liked this idea of every time they arrive back at a village it is like having long lost families reunion, everyone meeting up after a long absence, he felt part of it, and he liked that feeling very much indeed.

The next day everyone was summoned to the meeting hut, Peter walked in with Marcella and Carl, Vinchenzo and the rest of the men where already gathered, "right men as you know we part company here! Those of you who are guardian must return to "Point Zero", the rest of us to our appointed places of work, so we must part company."

Peter looked at Marcella and the look of sadness in his eyes, cheer up Marcella Peter said, "we are going home to Rome."

Marcella looked at Peter and said, "no Peter, you are going home I can't come with you his time."

"What do you mean you can't come with me, you live their as well?"

"Not anymore" said Vinchenzo and he took Peter to one side, "Peter there's something you need to know!"

Peter looked alarmed by this stage, "wh-what do I need to know?" he said with a lump in his throat,

Vinchenzo told Peter to sit down, Peter sat in a rocking chair near the open fire, Vinchenzo and Marcella began to explain Marcella' situation to him, Peter Vinchenzo said, "Marcella has change, he's not the Marcella you knew any more."

Peter said "what do you mean of course he is?"

"No! Peter I'm not" said Marcella.

Peter replied "well how are you different? I know I can drive you two mad with my coffee, but I can change honest!"

Marcella and Vinchenzo smiled, "no Peter its nothing to do with you at all."

Peter sat in the chair the tears trickling down his cheeks, "I want you to come home with me all of you!"

"That's not possible any more Peter!" said Marcella "I can't ever return to my former life, you see Peter, when we were in the castle I passed over from mortality to immortality, I died and was resurrected, I can't leave this place until I am needed again, but I will always be at your side in spirit, even though not in body you will always know I'm there with you close at hand I promise!"

Peter looked at Marcella, the tears running from his eyes, "he said promise!"

Marcella, smiled "I told you I promise."

Peter looked towards Vinchenzo, "are you to stay too Father Vinchenzo?"

"Oh, goodness me no I'll still be working with you in Rome, except this time you will be in charge of the office and I'll be occupying Monsignor Gazelle' office as I'm sure he won't object."

Peter looked at Vinchenzo and said "I've known in my heart and I think I always have that on our return all would not be the same, just give me time to accept all that has happened."

The men agreed and left Peter by the side of the fire, Peter held on tight to his favourite old mug, which by now he had filled with his favourite coffee, he thought about what had been said, then he thought how lucky he was to have such good friends, and Peter thanked God for the extra time he had with Marcella, Peter wiped his eyes and rejoined the group, Carl put his arm around Peter in a comforting way and squeezing him, he smiled and whispered, "don't worry Peter I'll look after Marcella and we'll both look after you!"

This gave Peter great comfort to know Marcella would not be alone, Peter liked Carl and felt he could trust him with his life if need be.

Vinchenzo began "right men those of us going back to reality, the plane awaits, for those staying, farewell until the next time we meet."

The men all hugged each other then headed for the plane, Peter walked slowly with Marcella, "goodbye Marcella."

Marcella replied "goodbye Peter, and don't worry we'll meet up again soon" he said.

Peter once again had a tear in his eye as he boarded the plane, he stood in the doorway and turned to wave but Marcella had gone, and so had the village all he could see was snow and ice for as far as the eye could see, Peter looked up at Vinchenzo, and said "where is everybody! and where's the village?"

"Oh its still there Peter but you can't see it anymore, however, they can still see you, the village and its residents are not visible because we have no need of them now, but you'll see them again one day, I'm sure of that, there are many things hidden from man in this life, for if he really knew what was on this earth, he would just destroy himself to obtain its beauty."

Peter boarded the plane and they took off this time there was to be no adventure, it was homeward bound, the men were to be dropped off a various points on the way and finally Peter and Vinchenzo would head back to a somewhat ordinary life, Peter wasn't sure if he could handle mundane life again after what he had just been through, but he thought what else was left, he would have to adjust himself to everyday living.

Peter and Vinchenzo returned to Rome and Peter took up his new job as head of department and continued to work for several months, he visited Vinchenzo as often as he could to hear the news of how well Marcella was doing, Peter had two new young assistants now, Angela and Bridget, two lovely if not rowdy young ladies, Peter had his hands full with these two, they reminded him of Marcella and himself when they first began to work for Vinchenzo, he told Vinchenzo of his two assistant, Vinchenzo replied well I wonder who that reminds you of? and both men began to laugh, Peter felt Marcella was laughing with them.

The next few months passed quickly and before long it was a year since he and Vinchenzo had returned home from his epic adventure, he still had fond memories of his time with Marcella and the others, yes there were times when he feared for his life but that was masked by the fun times, he'd forgotten about the sleepless nights and the perilous danger they had been in at times, they were memories he didn't care to remember, but he fondly remembered the nights around the camp fires, where, he and Marcella had laughed and joked about his addiction to coffee.

While Peter was reminiscing in his office over a nice cup of coffee, the door opened and in walked Angelo, Peter sat up straight in his chair, the coffee almost shooting out of his hand, the hairs on the back of his neck stood on end, he felt the rush of adrenalin enter his body, he dare not breath.

Angelo approached him, he had a crumpled piece of paper in his hand, Peters eye brow lifted, a smile came to his face, he felt that school boy feeling of mischief and excitement come over himself just like it did that year or so ago, "hello Angelo long time no see?"

Angelo smiled in a mischievous way, "yes he said I know what you mean", he handed Peter the piece of crumpled up paper, Peter held it for a second or two, he could feel the electricity from the paper, he knew, he just knew things were about to get exciting once again, he opened the paper up and sure enough it was a small map on the top of which was wrote I've found the grail, dated September the fourth 1841 John Fletcher, Peter quickly headed for a filing cabinet, he opened it up and scraped through the files until he came to a file that said John Fletcher lost expedition to Malta, Peter quickly opened it , inside was a file reporting that John Fletcher was a explorer who had set off after the grail, he was thought lost in a storm at sea somewhere off the island Malta, but was never heard of again, Peter cried "Eureka!" and slammed the draw shut, Angela and Bridget ran over to Peter, "are you alright?" they said.

Peter, looked over at them "oh, yes, yes! I'm fine", he said with a look of smugness on his face, Peter then walked over to Angelo, "where did you find this?"

Angelo smiled and as he turned to leave the room he looked back and winked at Peter saying, "you know where I found it", a shiver of anticipation came over Peter as he thought here we go again, he quickly grabbed his coat and said to the girls "I'll be out of the office for the rest of the day, come around to mine this evening at six o'clock."

Angela and Bridget looked at each other in a bewildered way, they acknowledged Peters request and Peter headed out of the door as if he was running to a fire, the girls just shook their heads, "what was that all about?" said Angela.

Bridget replied, "I'm not sure but whatever it was it most certainly caught Peters attention, I'm sure all will be revealed tonight when we meet him at home."

"Well" Angela said "whatever all this is about it caused Peter to leave his coffee still untouched, and that in my book is serious stuff, he never leaves his coffee, he drinks it first, this is worrying indeed."

Peter ran over to Vinchenzo' office, he burst in, "Father Vinchenzo, Father Vinchenzo! he exclaimed in an excitable voice!"

Vinchenzo looked up from his desk, and said "Peter, its Monsignor now."

Peter, looked at Vinchenzo, with a sheepish style look and said "very quietly, sorry, Father, I mean your eminence."

Vinchenzo replied that's alright Peter, then he winked and Peter smiled, he told Peter to slow down, then said, "now Peter, what's the matter, he said?"

Peter was all at sea with excitement, Vinchenzo told Peter once more to calm down, "what has got you so excited?"

Peter took several deep breaths then looked at Vinchenzo and said "I need to go and visit Father Angus in Bonn!"

Vinchenzo' eye brow lifted and a smile appeared on his face, "do you real! now that's interesting, and may one ask "why?"

Peter showed Vinchenzo the map, Vinchenzo' face lit up, he said "I'll alert the necessary people, go now Peter, I'll be in touch shortly, meanwhile find out what you can."

"Yes" Father Peter replied, then squinted and clicking his fingers, turn back towards Vinchenzo, "sorry I meant Monsignor."

Vinchenzo smiled and said "that's alright Peter, now go! and go quickly."

Peter kissed the Monsignors hand, and returned home, to await further orders, thinking to himself the games afoot once more, I can't wait to see Marcella and the others again.

The End
(Until next time that is)

About the Author:

Georgina Thomas is a pen name of the author, the author was brought up in the nineteen fifties, in the Northeast of England coming from a rather large family and has been married thirty four years and has two children, as well as a grandson, with a further grand child due any day now, the author now lives and works in their native Northeast, as a Pastor in a church plant in Whitburn, Nr Sunderland Tyne and Wear.

Printed in the United States
62258LVS00003B/262-279